VIDA

VIDA

PATRICIA ENGEL

Black Cat
a paperback original imprint of Grove/Atlantic, Inc.
New York

Portions of this book have appeared in slightly different form in the following publications: "Lucho" in *Boston Review,* "Refuge" in *Story Quarterly,* "Green" in *Sycamore Review,* "Desaliento" in *Boston Review,* "Paloma" in *Fourteen Hills,* "Cielito Lindo" in *Driftwood,* "Vida" in *Harpur Palate,* "Día" in *Guernica,* and "Madre Patria" in *Quarterly West.*

Published simultaneously in Canada
Printed in the United States of America

FIRST EDITION

ISBN: 978-0-8021-7078-1

Black Cat
a paperback original imprint of Grove/Atlantic, Inc.
841 Broadway
New York, NY 10003

Distributed by Publishers Group West

www.groveatlantic.com

10 11 12 13   10 9 8 7 6 5 4 3 2

Everything is for my parents

CONTENTS

Lucho   1

Refuge   23

Green   45

Desaliento   59

Paloma   77

Cielito Lindo   103

Vida   117

Día   147

Madre Patria   157

In each life, particularly at its dawn,
there exists an instant
which determines everything.

—Jean Grenier, *Islands*

LUCHO

It was the year my uncle got arrested for killing his wife, and our family was the subject of all the town gossip. My dad and uncle were business partners, so my parents were practically on trial themselves, which meant that most of the parents didn't want their kids to hang around me anymore, and I lost the few friends I had.

We were foreigners, spics, in a town of blancos. I don't know how we ended up there. There's tons of Latinos in New Jersey, but somehow we ended up in the one town that only kept them as maids. All the kids called me brownie on account of my permanent tan, or Indian because all the Indians they saw on TV were dark like me. I thought the gringos were all pink, not white, but I never said so. I was a quiet kid. Lonely, and a hell of a lot lonelier once my family became the featured topic on the nightly news.

That's how I took up with Lucho. He moved to our block with his mom when she married the bachelor doctor who lived in the big house on the hill. Lucho had a Spanish name because his mom was living with an Argentinean guy when she had him, but Lucho's dad was someone else. Some other guy who came and went with the sunrise.

He was sixteen and I was fourteen, which meant we could be friends on our block but had to ignore each other at school. He had squishy lips and a small round nose, smooth shiny skin, and greasy dark hair. All the girls checked him out. But Lucho was kind of dirty for a town like ours. He always wore the same thing: faded jeans with holes around the pockets and a white button-down shirt that looked like it only got washed in the sink. He was sort of tall, taller than me at least, and skinny the way boys are till they discover beer. He smoked cigarettes and sat around on patches of grass on the school grounds, sort of taking it all in. The other guys didn't talk to him, except the loser kids who are always the first to befriend someone new. Lucho wasn't interested though.

He discovered me without my knowing it. One day he came knocking on our front door. My mom never answered the door or the phone. She went into this depression with the whole trial, was always crying, seeing the shrink, talking about how we should just move to Italy so we could go to museums all day instead of having to deal with people calling us immigrant criminals all the time. Usually when the doorbell rang it was a reporter wanting a statement, or a neighbor with the newspaper wrapped in a paper bag. Our maid didn't answer the door anymore either because Papi said the last thing we need is people coming down on us for hiring illegals.

So I answered it and Lucho was standing there, looking bored on our front steps. I saw him once or twice on the block, knew he moved in and that he made some people nervous. He looked at me like we knew each other for a while already and said, "Why don't you come for a walk with me by the river?"

"Do you even know my name?" I asked him, which I guess was a dumb thing to say, but you know how it is when you get caught off guard.

He gave me that look, like I was a silly kid and he was just going to endure me. He didn't say anything, just stood there and waited. I shouted to my mom upstairs that I'd be back later, and she didn't respond, so I walked out the door. It wasn't until I stepped on the concrete that I realized I was barefoot, but I kept walking and followed him to the river in the woods at the end of the block.

When we were there he started smoking like an old pro, which I thought was impressive because, around here, they card you to buy smokes and nobody has the nerve to break any kind of rules. It's a town full of wusses, a polo-shirt army of numbnuts.

"This town fuckin' blows," he said, and I was kind of scared of him because my mom always told me that when you're alone with a guy, he could totally kill you. I mean, look at my poor tía who got strangled by her own husband.

"I think I'm gonna go," I started to say, and Lucho looked at me like I was a waste of time.

"Don't be such a baby," he said. "I'm not gonna do anything to you." Then he started to crack up.

"Besides, you'd be the wrong chick to mess with. I hear your uncle's a killer."

That was the first time anyone ever said that to me, and I felt a little pride in it. I smiled. Can you believe it?

"So whatcha gonna do when you get out of this place?"

"I don't know," I said, because it was the only place I knew. "College?"

"College is for pussies. You gotta get out there and live, Sabina."

I don't know who told him my name. Probably the same people who told him about my family. I didn't say anything and he stopped talking, just sat there and smoked while we stared out at the shallow river. This river used to be full of trout. Now it was just a stream of sludge and mud. My feet were covered in the stuff, and there was a huge beetle crawling up my leg. I let it hop onto my finger and showed it to Lucho. He smiled at the little green creature, took it onto his fingertip and stuck it in his mouth, crunching down. He stuck his naked tongue out at me to show me he'd really eaten it.

Of course they found my uncle guilty of murder. He was always saying he was innocent, that someone framed him, even suggested that my dad set him up so he'd get the whole company, but nobody bought it. We knew he was guilty because that's the kind of guy my uncle was. Always smacking the shit out of his wife, so that my mom would have to take her to the hospital and let her stay at our house until the two of them finally made up again. My uncle would show up with jewelry or a new car and she'd eat it up. And once or twice my uncle turned to me and whispered some dark shit like, "You see, mi amor, all women are whores for money."

My mom really hated my uncle. She said I wasn't allowed to be in a room alone with him. I said, "Mom, if he ever hits me I'll stab him." She said it wasn't him hitting me that she was afraid of.

Now it was the business of the sentencing. Life or death. We're Catholic and officially against the death penalty, but I won't lie: I think we all knew we'd be better off with my uncle underground. The next step was that he was going to be sued by his dead wife's family for every penny he had, which was actually every penny my dad had, due to their

7

shared business interests. Mami was freaking. She knew Papi was going to be paying off that murder for the rest of his life, and then she started cursing Papi, saying how she always told him going into business with my uncle was a big mistake.

I was telling all this to Lucho one day. We were sitting on the front steps of my house, me drinking a Coke and him smoking. My mom thought Lucho was sucio, but she was glad I had a friend, although she kept telling me not to let him kiss me, and I was embarrassed because my mom has this thing where she thinks every guy is trying to seduce you.

Then this car pulled up in front of my house and this skinny lady, with red hair and a blue linen dress that was so see-through in the sunlight that we could make out her lace panties and everything, came wobbling up the hill in her cheap heels. She stopped right in front of us and looked nervous. She was carrying a leather folder stuffed with papers, and she looked like she had a ton she was waiting to say.

She asked if this was the right house and Lucho said, "Who wants to know."

"You must be Sabina?" She looked like she was trying hard to be warm. "I'm a friend of your uncle's. I'm writing a book about his struggle with the legal system and his unlawful incarceration."

Oh, no. Not one of those locas my uncle manages to screw and brainwash to become his crusaders. He's got this talent for converting any kind of woman, be it one of his female lawyers or his former cleaning lady, making her fall in love with him and be willing to give her whole life away just so she can give him blowjobs in the visitors' room at the jail and write letters to the governor on his behalf. I know the part about the blowjobs because I heard my mom telling her sister in Colombia about it with major disgust one day.

"You know there's like five other chicks writing books already," I told her. "You better think of something new to say."

She looked hurt and I almost felt bad for her. I always feel bad for dumb women. Don't ask me why.

"He's a wife beater, not a serial killer. Pretty fuckin' simple. Asshole killer. Period." That was Lucho talking. He was a really good wingman.

"So how do you know my uncle?" I asked her, suddenly trying to be sort of nice because, really, I don't want anyone saying I have bad manners.

She wouldn't say. She started fumbling with her folder, took out a pen, and said she wanted to ask me some questions, that she knew me from when I was little and she and my uncle were friends for a long time.

"No way," I told her.

"She's not answering shit without her lawyer present." Again, that was Lucho.

The lady looked amused. "He your boyfriend?"

"I'm the watchdog, bitch. Now get off this property before we call the cops on your slut ass and give you a real fuckin' reason to write a book." Lucho didn't even raise his voice. He said it cool, calm, like he was ordering a pizza, and the lady in the see-through dress looked like she was going to have a heart attack. She started walking off on her rickety legs, almost tripping on the stone path back to her car.

You know, I was kind of a late bloomer. I was playing with Barbies till I was thirteen, way later than normal, and believe me, it was hard to give them up, because I loved the freedom of the Barbie world, making up stories for their skinny bodies. I never really got into liking boys much, even when girls my age were getting boyfriends and going to the movies with them and stuff. Boys didn't like me much either. Lucho was cute, though, and I started to think I might like him in that way, but every time I started to think about what it would be like to kiss him, I got nervous around him, and I hated that feeling, so I pushed it all out of my mind.

One day he said I was pretty but shouldn't act pretty because that's not attractive at all. I knew he had a thing going on with this eleventh-grade girl named Courtney whose mom sold us our house and whose dad owned the car dealership in town. Courtney was blonde and blow-dried her hair for no reason. She got manicures and wore makeup that never melted, even in gym class, which we had at the same time. She had an official boyfriend, who played lacrosse and was a senior on his way to Lehigh like everyone else in this town, but she and Lucho snuck around the graveyard together, and he told me that she even laid her naked boobs down on the headstone of some Dutch settler and then laughed like a madwoman.

This made me uncomfortable. I pretended to be really busy retying my shoe when Lucho was telling me the details of making out with her behind the old colonial church. I reminded him she had a boyfriend, and he was like, "Who cares? It's not like I wanna marry her."

We were lying in the grass in my backyard. My mom was on the phone with Colombia, like usual, and my dad was at court, like usual.

"Hey, don't you have a brother?" Lucho rolled over on his belly. He had a blade of grass between his teeth and the sun made his cheeks red and spotty.

"He's at boarding school."

"You never talk about him."

"I forget he exists."

"That's fucked."

"I know."

"You want to make out?"

He was lying there, propped up on one elbow, squinting the sun out of his eyes. His hair was extra greasy today and he stunk a little. I wondered how often he showered. I showered twice a day because my mom had an insane sense of smell and was always telling me she could smell my dirty pits.

"My mom can totally see us from her bedroom window," I said.

"So let's go to my house. The doc took my mom to the city. No one's home."

I started shaking my head, but I was smiling.

"Come on, Sabina. You know you want to."

You know how it is when you're a teenager. Just when things start getting good, your mom calls you in for some urgent bullshit reason like your aunt is on the phone and wants to ask if you liked the crap she sent you for your birthday.

My mom loved her shopping trips. She gave up smoking when she had me, and she never drank. Clothes were her thing, and my role was to sit on the chair in the dressing room and tell her whether or not my father would like the outfit, because if Papi didn't like something, she'd take it right back the next day. Lucho came along once, which was sort of funny. While my mom searched the racks, Lucho and I wandered into the panties and bras section, and he held up a sexy bustier and told me I had stuff like that to look forward to when my boobs came in. He stayed for dinner at our house a lot, and that evening, as we ate, my mom started asking Lucho how his mom met the doctor, and he got all flustered, like he was in trouble or something.

"I'm not supposed to say, but they met through an ad in the paper."

"What paper?" I swear, my mom is so nosy sometimes.

"Well, not really a paper. It was an agency kind of thing."

I kicked my mom under the table so she'd stop asking questions, but she gave me this look like it was her house and her right to ask whatever she wanted.

I only knew that Lucho and his mom lived in California before coming to Jersey. She was living with another guy out there. A Mexican who sold horses and taught Lucho how to ride. Lucho said he wasn't so bad, but that he threw them out one day and they had to find a new situation.

"Have you thought about college yet?" This was my mom's favorite question to any kid over ten. All new-money immigrants have a thing about American colleges.

"Yeah, I'm not going. The doc says I gotta work. I think I'm going back to California to be an actor."

"What does your mother say about that?"

"That I gotta leave when I'm eighteen." He turned to me and then to my mom. "I'm taking Sabina with me."

My mom laughed, but I knew she thought he was being fresh. Fresh enough to ban from our house from here on out.

"Oh no you're not," Mami hummed. "Sabina is staying right here with us."

I hated school. Even the teachers were whispering about my family's place in the news. How my grandparents had to beg the judge to spare my uncle's life. How my uncle had a couple of illegitimate kids around the state. And then all the gruesome details of the murder itself, which my mom was careful to keep from me. She attended the trial on most days and alternated which side of the courtroom she sat on. She always came home sullen, and when I asked her what happened that day, she said it was better I didn't know.

Lucho and I were sitting by the river, which was almost dried up and it wasn't even summer yet. We sat side by side on this old tree that curves over the river, growing sideways like a cripple, our feet swinging in the air. Lucho was smoking. One day I asked him how he bought cigarettes without getting in trouble, and he said the doctor bought them for him. I thought it was pretty cool of him to do that for Lucho, treat him like an adult like that.

He never tried to make out with me. We were just sitting there, listening to the crickets and flicking the ants off our thighs, when out of nowhere Lucho goes, "I heard your uncle raped that lady before he killed her."

"My aunt, you mean."

"Yeah."

I shrugged because I had heard that before—I heard my mom tell it to her sister on the phone—but I didn't understand how you could be raped by someone you were already married to.

"You ever been raped?" Lucho asked me.

"No."

"Not even molested?"

"No."

"Not even a little bit when you were a kid? Your brother never tried to feel your tits or anything?"

"Ew! No!" I was laughing. My brother was a total computer nerd till he got sent away because he fell into a bad crowd.

"Not even by someone else's dad at the town pool or anything?"

"Lucho . . . you're such a perv."

"I'm just asking."

He got quiet, and then I felt kind of bad for calling him a pervert. He threw his cigarette stub into the dry soil and lit a new one right away.

The way the court arranged it, my dad could buy my uncle out of his half of the company and make monthly payments that would go straight to the parents of his dead wife. My uncle got life in the slammer and Papi got thirty years of payments. And those people got a dead daughter. My mom said that on our end of it, it meant we had to watch our spending.

"Does this mean we can't afford to send me to college?"

"No," said Mami. "It means we're being audited by the IRS."

Summer vacation hadn't even started, and I already thought I was going to kill myself from overexposure to my parents. One Saturday, I went over to Lucho's and knocked on the door. His mom answered. She was a nice-looking lady with fake blonde hair and a tan that you know nobody is born with. She had some kind of accent. I asked Lucho where she was from, and he said she's a Jew, which means she's from everywhere. Bulgaria. Denmark. Turkey. Israel. A bunch of places.

Her name was Shula, and the thing I liked best about her was that she let me call her Shula, not Mrs. Whatever like all the other stiff moms in town. My mom was a first-name kind of lady, too, and it wigged out all my friends when she told them to just call her Maria. Shula waved me in and told me Lucho was out by the pool, so I trekked through the doctor's fancy house and found him under an umbrella, shirt off, wearing cutoff jeans I'd never seen before. He was stringy and tan, and then I saw them. Scars all over his arms, long welts and bruises on his back, and a big bruise on his chest.

"Lucho, what happened to you?"

"The doc kicks the shit out of me." He laughed.

My parents never laid a finger on us, even when my brother made my mom cry, which was often.

"What does your mom say about it?"

"She tells him not to but he doesn't listen."

Just then Shula came out and said she had to go to the mall and that she'd bring us back some Kentucky Fried if we wanted. We said okay and when it seemed like she was really gone, Lucho stood up, peeled off his shorts, and jumped in the pool. I caught a glimpse of his wiry behind, the shadows of his groin, and I swallowed hard. It was the first time I saw a boy naked in real life except for babies and once when my brother left the bathroom door unlocked.

"I don't have my bathing suit, Lucho."

"So take your clothes off."

I don't know what came over me but I started peeling off my clothes right there, dropping my shirt, then my shorts, onto the plastic lounge chair. I was down to my underwear, some pink cotton ones my mom bought with a matching pink bra. I was unhooking the bra when Shula reappeared, looking like she forgot something, setting her eyes on me and her naked son in the pool.

"Sabina, I think you'd better go."

"I forgot my bathing suit . . ."

"Go now, please."

I got dressed quick-style and flew down the block to my house, terrified that Shula was going to call my mom and tell her I was trying to get naked in her house, but then it occurred to me that if she did such a thing, I could just shoot back that her husband beat the crap out of Lucho and that would shut her up good.

That night I heard clanking on my window while I lay in bed thinking about Lucho's stinky naked body and how badly I wanted to see it again. I went over and opened it and saw him in the shadows of our yard, flinging his sneaker up at my window.

"Hey, I got the doc's car! Come on, I'll take you for a ride!"

I probably would have jumped right out the window if it hadn't been for the fact that two years earlier when my brother was fifteen, he tried to sneak out of his own bedroom window next to mine to go to a party and broke his collarbone in the process. Our neighbors heard him screaming before we did and called the police. I told Lucho to wait for me. I hadn't taken three steps out of my room when I heard my mom call out to me, "Sabina? Are you going to the kitchen?"

Fuck. I told her yes, and she told me to bring her a glass of water. Lucho met me by the back door, and I told him I couldn't go anywhere with him. I was standing there in my nightshirt, one that my dad got me on a business trip. It had a big fat cat on it and HONG KONG printed across the chest. The maid shrank it so it barely covered my butt.

"You look cute," Lucho said. "Want to sneak me into your room?"

"My dad will kill me if we get caught."

"Fuck it. Your dad doesn't hit for shit."

"I'll be grounded."

"So what? You never go anywhere anyway."

"Lucho . . ."

"Okay, you give me no choice. I gotta go throw my sneakers at Courtney's window now."

This made me jealous. Courtney with her hot ballet body and country-club tan. The country club where they only let in Mayflower people. I told Lucho how they didn't let Jews in there either and he laughed and said Courtney lets Jews in, no problem.

He left, and I got my mother her glass of water, crept across the creaky floors, and went to sleep with the window open.

My mother came into my room that morning and told me, just like that, you don't have to go to school today if you don't want to, Sabina. Something terrible happened last night.

Lucho drove into the highway divider. No car got in his way, nothing pushed him in that direction. It was just one of those things. The poor kid lost control of the car, is how my dad put it. The poor kid. That's what everyone called him. Most people didn't even know his name because he was still so new to the town. But everyone in school put on a sad face, went to see the guidance counselors, and took advantage of the school's lenient attendance policy for poststudent deaths. I went to my classes.

Then there was the funeral. You'd never guess it but kids love a funeral when it's for one of their own. They dress up in black, and the girls cluster together and cry, cry, cry like preemies. All the parents came, too, showed support, and looked concerned, although nobody really gave a fuck. Lucho was the good-looking smelly kid, the one all the moms said needed a shower. The one who lived with the rich doctor who, with all his loot, wouldn't buy his new stepson some new clothes. The doc looked really upset at the funeral, and Shula sat there crying her eyes out. The casket was closed, though I'm not sure if it's a Jewish thing or because he was so mangled from the wreck.

My brother stole my dad's car years earlier and went on the highway, got pulled over, arrested, and sentenced to a million hours of washing fire trucks with a sponge. That was reason enough to keep to the back roads. My Lucho never had a chance.

What's worse is that at the funeral, people got distracted by the sight of my parents and the whispers started. Every detail of my dad's payout to my uncle and the victim's family had been offered up by the stupid local papers that always implied Papi was a trafficker. My mother was dressed to kill, as always, in some designer getup that was way too much for a town like this where all the mothers were doughier versions of their husbands.

I sat between my parents at the funeral. Mami cried, but she cries for anything nowadays. I think she felt bad because, just the week before, she told me Lucho looked like a criminal waiting to happen. My father held my head close to his chest and kissed my hair. "He was a nice kid, Sabina. He knew you loved him."

Papi surprised me. I didn't even know I loved Lucho till that second. But I did. Because so what if he was a little smelly and weird. He came looking for me when I was invisible. And when he was with me, he acted like I was the only thing he could see.

Courtney didn't come to the funeral because people said she was way too emotional, which I didn't really buy. I thought she got more attention than if she actually showed up and had to sit in the rows of chairs with the rest of us. This rabbi came out and said some Hebrew prayer. I heard kids giggling behind me. I thought of Lucho and how he'd say that was fucked.

REFUGE

This morning the towers were hit and I was in bed—not at the office in Tower One—because I called in sick again. My brother phoned, said turn on the TV, and I watched it all, everything I don't need to describe now. Before the phones went dead, I made contact. Parents, a few friends. Trying to decide how to handle this mess, but I'm in no position to make a decision, which is a good thing because Luscious Lou (his stage name), my guitar teacher of these past few months, showed up at my door, all seven feet of him in his usual black leather and suede, leaning on the frame, that sleeping crow of hair on his head, diagonal nose like a dragon's tail, tiny gray eyes folded into hard wrinkles. Moist, bellowing voice: "Sabina, I knew you'd be home."

He told me to go with him, that I live too close to the scene. I packed some clothes and followed him down to the street, his massive hand pulling mine. My neighbors, my party people, all out on the stoop with eyes like this day might last forever. For a second I felt I finally belonged to this city—the broken-down horizon matched my bombed-out heart.

I don't know why Lou, of all people, came for me. The whole long walk up to his place on Riverside Drive—trains were paralyzed—I kept thinking how I wished Nico had been at the door instead. Last I heard, he was in L.A. doing his musician thing. Probably not doing so well, because, I can say this now, Nico's not really that talented. Didn't change the way I loved him, though—like he was some kind of genius—and maybe that's why he started to act like I was lucky to be with him. It made him hard to be around sometimes. But those lashes. They could split your will into shards.

I'm at Lou's house, which is really the house his wife inherited from her deceased first husband. When he brought me here, he introduced me to her and the kids as his favorite student. The wife, Olive, is striking: equal parts Snow White and Nancy Wilson. A cocktail of a woman small enough to fit in Lou's jacket pocket. She looks at me like I'm a sick person, pitying and fearful of catching what I've got. She has still, glossy Valium eyes and floats around the house like a spirit while the toddler twin boys roll Tonka trucks on the shag carpet, Lou makes burgers, and I sit on the sofa with Sierra, the thirteen-year-old daughter leftover from the first marriage. She's fat-faced but thin of body, greasy-haired with a nest of chin pimples covered in drugstore foundation, the kind I used to stuff up my sleeves along with nail polish and lipsticks with my junior-high friend Alina. We never got caught, but somehow I've always felt guilty, and when I go to drugstores now I want to walk up to the cashier and say, Look, I didn't steal anything.

I'm not good with young people, or any people, really, so I ask Sierra what she wants to be when she grows up.

"A stripper, because they make a lot of money."

I ask if her parents know and she looks at me like I'm an idiot. Asks me what I do for a living, and I think, I'm only twenty-two. I don't do anything for a living except smoke cigarettes and throw my heart around. What I've got is a job, not a living.

"I'm a receptionist at an investment bank."

Her eyes lower, mockingly. "Is that your dream come true?"

I could say investment banks happen to pay very well, but instead I try to sound adult and unaffected. "Actually, I'm looking to make a career change."

I can't help focusing on her clothes. Tight low jeans. A ratty blue tank with BABYGIRL painted in shiny stones across her cupcake-size boobies.

She wants to know about my love life.

27

"Do you have a boyfriend, Sabrina?"

I tell her it's Sabina, not Sabrina, and I'm single, which sounds corny, like I'm on a dating show, and I wonder why Sierra is talking like she's my social worker.

"Were you a virgin when you were thirteen?"

I'm trying not to embarrass us both, so I answer her as if I get asked that question at least once a day.

"I was. Yes."

"I'm not. I've had sex with four guys already."

She goes on about how the guys were older, like eighteen. I've got one eye on the tots on the rug, wondering if they'll register any part of this conversation.

Another dumb question: I ask if she was in love with any of the guys, as if love is the reason everyone does the things they do.

"No. I kind of love this guy who lives on the third floor, but he's married. Besides, I think he likes my mom, because he hangs around here a lot when Lou is in the studio. Or at your house."

Nico thought it was strange that Lou would come over for lessons after midnight and that the one-hour lesson would extend to two or three. I explained that Lou had a packed recording schedule and his only available slots were late at night, which suited me fine since I was a recent insomniac. Nico didn't like that I was learning to play. I'd asked him to teach me himself a hundred times, but he always refused, so I had no choice but to find myself a teacher, and it happened that the guy who cuts my hair knew of Luscious Lou because his own wife took lessons from him.

"You just don't want me to learn," I said.

Nico shook his head. "You're the one they say is unteachable."

This was a personal jab—Nico's area of expertise—because I'd confided in him that as a kid, I had shit skills for music. The same teacher who deemed my brother a musical prodigy said I was hopeless, which I thought meant homeless, and then my mother had to explain the difference to me. In elementary school, I couldn't string together three notes on the recorder. In sixth grade, I was told to quit the clarinet, and when I tried out for the school choir, I was told to leave it to the girls with smooth, far-reaching voices.

By the time I linked up with Lou, Nico and I were already headed for trouble. But there were nights when I was in bed with Nico and I'd get up to answer the door and strum chords with Lou for hours while my man slept. I'd written lyrics for Nico to set to music, but he wouldn't even look at them, so I gave them to Lou. One night, I had wet lashes, not unusual, because Nico kept me in a state of panic. Lou looked at my sheets of paper and said, "Lets turn those wet eyes into music," and we spent the whole night drawing melodies over chords until it sounded like a real song.

It always seemed like Lou didn't want to go home and I never asked why, because people have their own reasons and God knows that for most of my life, home is the last place I wanted to be. Yet our lessons always felt like stolen time. When Lou left, I'd get back into bed with Nico. He'd feel me slip under the covers, reach for me, bend his head into my chest, curl into my torso for the length of the night. But in the morning his eyes would shift to derision and he'd say, "This is all wrong. We are all wrong." And one day, he was gone.

After dinner, Lou reads the boys a story and stays with them until they fall asleep in their little twin beds with Snoopy sheets and padded side rails. I used to have rails like that as a kid, but I still fell out of bed all the time, landing on the rug with a thud, and sometimes I waited a long time to see if either of my parents would come running to make sure I was okay but they rarely did. Sometimes my brother would appear, because his room was just next to mine and our shared wall was as thin as tissue, even my sneezes would wake him, and Cris was very protective of his sleep. I'd be on the floor, wrapped in my blanket and looking like a runny enchilada with the bed bumper on top of me, but he wouldn't do anything to help me.

Lou and the wife keep talking about how lucky I am that I called in sick or I might be dead right now. Lou, who has become very religious since he turned fifty, says I should say a prayer of thanks and go light some candles at St. Patrick's or something. He used to play with Bowie, Dylan, the Stones, all the greats. He told me he's slept with a million women, done every drug under the sun, and it was all for nothing; at the end of the day that shit has nothing to do with music. Now Lou mostly records studio tracks for these young bands from Brooklyn, but he says they don't have the heart needed to live music. It's all about the heart, says Lou. The bloodier the heart, the better the music.

We've been watching the news since the kids went to sleep. Those images of people covered in dust. The repeated loop of the towers collapsing like a deflated carnival castle. I think of all my coworkers, people I never really took the trouble to know. Shalonie, the Jamaican mommy of two who worked the reception desk with me. All the horny banker guys would say, "Shalonie is so pretty. It's too bad she's all crooked," just because one of her legs is shorter than the other and half of her drags when she walks. I hope she made it down the stairs okay.

And Wanda Rios, the HR lady who looked out for me when the executive assistants got together to complain that I should be fired because I take one-hour lunches—more than my allotted twenty minutes—and read fashion magazines on the job. The Polish girl before me was way more serious and responsible, but she got promoted to accounting. Wanda likes me because we have the same last name though we are no relation—she's Puerto Rican and I'm Colombian stock— and she says us Latinos have to stick together although she doesn't speak Spanish.

These are people who had it in them to be faithful servants of the bank, hoping for holiday bonuses, a little recognition, and eventually a promotion, while I spent my days trying to get fired. Their survival is certainly worth more than mine. It's hard to feel grateful knowing I should have been with them today. And that I cheated.

I can't help thinking of Nico. I picture him sweaty and tan, every bit the rocker, sitting in some Silverlake bar watching the news over a beer, telling the people around him how he used to live right there, that his girl worked right there in the towers. I wonder if he's worried about me and if, under that, there's a trace of something more.

The last time I used the word *terrorist* in normal conversation was when I called Nico an emotional terrorist for missing my college graduation because he took his ex to get an abortion and told me to stop being so selfish. Never mind that the news byte came from her, not him. The baby was his—the result of what he called an *isolated incident*. He managed to convince me not to give up on him, on us, even if for a while we weren't rapturous lovers but more like two slabs of beef in a meat locker.

Does it really matter how we met? Why is that always the first question people ask? I was at a crosswalk on Lower Broadway when Nico flew by on his bike and his handlebar caught my purse strap, pulling me down into a puddle. He stopped to check if I was injured, but I received him with a blazing "Are you trying to kill me?" He balanced on his bike while some strangers helped me up, apologizing while I yelled that he was a hazard to society. Somehow we ended up kissing on the same street corner an hour later, after he'd bought me some deli roses and chocolates from Dean & Deluca.

My girlfriends considered Nico a big deal because he had gigs all over town, which might be one reason I stuck with him so long. Spaghetti-limbed, wet-lipped, and moody, broke but with the good looks and arrogance of a young hustler, as if his pockets were packed with bills. Nico, all bravado, even had my parents in the thrall of his rising star.

He didn't smoke, but I did, and when I'd put a stem to my lips, he'd rip it from my mouth and toss it to the curb as if we were performing theater—two people playing the part of a lovelorn couple. For my birthday Nico had my name tattooed on his neck, which was a beautiful gesture that became tiresome because he'd throw it in my face whenever we fought, pointing to his jugular, screaming, "This is how much I love you!"

I couldn't tell any of this stuff to my family and friends or they'd think Nico and I were a pair of maniacs. But Lou listened to my stories without judging while he taught me how to fingerpick "Europa" and the song slowly came to life. When I was through he'd say, "You really love that son of a gun, don'tcha, Bean."

I thought I was lucky to live such a palpable love. A love you could spread out on a table or, in our case, take out with the garbage. Lou says Nico reminds him of himself when he was young and stupid and that he just needs a near-death experience to teach him what's what.

After hearing so much about us, Lou told me about him and Olive. How when he met her, he couldn't handle her because she was everything he ever wanted in a lady: smart, fucked-up, and beautiful. They slept together and then he ditched her and went on the road with some band. She got pregnant by another guy and married him. That was Sierra's daddy. Years later, Lou and Olive ran into each other at a wedding in Montauk. He convinced her to leave her man, but the guy died in a wreck before the divorce was final anyway. That's how she got the apartment. "Some love stories are just meant to be," said Lou. "You just have to let time do its thing."

He also told me the darker stuff. The antidepressants she often refused to take; pills meant to regulate her chemistry, keep her from hurting herself and her children. Sometimes she'd lock herself in her room for days and not even let Lou in. After an all-nighter at the studio, he sometimes found the boys in dirty clothes the next day—unbathed, unfed, crying, while Sierra did her best to keep them calm. Once or twice, she filled the house with gas from the stove, and the family survived by sheer luck and timing, which is why Lou says he's become so religious at this juncture in his life. The suicide attempts have mostly stopped. Now the tendency is toward epic silences and occasional flashes of homicidal rage during which she might chuck a butcher knife at Lou, leaving a hole in the wall that he'll eventually have to spackle.

Lou says Olive used to want to be an actress and people sometimes get loopy when their dreams don't pan out. Her first husband was on some old TV show that I've never heard of and did several pilots, but he was mostly unemployed at the end. Sometimes Lou suspects that Olive still loves him. "It's not her fault," he tells me. "The guy is dead. And death is a huge aphrodisiac."

* * *

A few hours in someone's home and you can smell the beast within. Lou, pulling his body around under the low roof, cleaning what the wife didn't clean, cooking what the wife didn't cook, while she watches, smoking cigarettes at the kitchen table.

"How long are we going to go on like this?" she says low enough to believe I can't hear from the next room.

He says he doesn't know what she means. They're a family. Families go through hard times. That's what they're designed for.

Then, just plates being washed. The rearranging of objects on the kitchen counter. I picture her rubbing out a cigarette in the clay ashtray one of the kids made her, ready to light another. His footsteps move closer to her. I feel them beside each other—see him put his hand on her shoulder. Hear him tell her, "She'll leave tomorrow."

Lou set me up on the sofa. Sheets, a pillow, a quilt with loose threads like dancing spiders. I won't sleep tonight even though his building is a monastery compared to my place down in the valley of nightclubs and fire stations. I haven't slept well in months. Ever since Nico started pulling unexplained absences. I'd ask, Where you been? And he'd say his family didn't flee Cuba so he could be oppressed by another regime, meaning me. I'm no beggar for love, despite what you might think, so I'd kick him out and he'd howl through the door how cruel I am, that I never loved him, that I don't know how to love because I'm a loveless, heartless panther who'd eat her own cubs, and I'd wonder who was this girl that he was talking about, because I knew she wasn't me.

These fights would go on till a neighbor called the police, till one of us quit, dropped to our knees in apology, till one of us began negotiating or proposed some semiplausible reconciliation plan, till we fell into each other again and admitted ownership as if there were no other choice but to keep this calamitous opera in production.

Just when I've beaten the night, I feel his arm on me. Lou shaking me from my half sleep, his muscular fingers tugging my skin. The darkness breaks with the glow of the street, spots of car lights on the walls, shining right through Lou so he looks as if he has a halo. He turns on a lamp. He's got a guitar hanging from a strap on his back and another, which he hands to me. I sit up, let the quilt become a pond around my waist. Take the guitar from him and run my fingertips over the fat metal strings.

I think maybe he wants to talk, but when I ask him what's wrong he puts his finger to his lips and shakes his head. We run through chord progressions. Play a few songs. In a couple of months, Lou has given me a small repertoire.

If you didn't know better, you might think I have talent. A real miracle worker, that Lou, teaching the unteachable.

We stay like this for a while. Lou, shirtless and shiny like porcelain, in black drawstring pajama pants, holding the guitar in his lap like a child. And me, in my university sweats, letting him lead me. Then I see Olive on the edge of the room like it's her curtain call and she's the sleeping princess who's come out for applause in her gauzy nightgown, sleepy-faced, pillow-bruised cheeks.

I stop my strumming and Lou looks behind him to see why.

I apologize for waking her, though I know that's not what she came for.

She doesn't say anything. Just stands there, and Lou gets up, tells me good night. He follows her down the hall and I hear the door click shut behind them.

Once we went to Coney Island and Nico got his teeth knocked out by some locals who didn't like his swagger. They were following us for a while, cooing that I had a hot ass and asking how much. When we were leaning on a railing sipping slushies, the guys came up close. Nico told them to fuck off and next thing you know they had him on the ground, his fly busted open, blood on his face, eyes shut like a smashed-up newborn. We were only together a few months by then, but that was the clincher. We'd laugh about it later, especially when his replacement teeth came loose or fell out while he was eating, say that that day was like a scene out of *The Warriors* and I was the girl in the leotard dress whose nipples are popping throughout the whole movie.

"The punches I took for you," Nico would say, like it was a debt to be paid.

I used to say: Why can't we be like normal people? Go to the bookstore, the movies, eat meals in restaurants and have conversations about things other than our latest love war, communicate in a language beyond screaming and screwing. We could be friends with other couples, have brunch, and hold hands at parties instead of eyeing each other like cannibals.

We could talk to each other, listen to each other.

We could teach each other things, make each other better people.

I used to say: I wish we met ten years from now. Maybe we could be something. Something other than what we are.

In the morning, I pretend to be asleep until the whole family is awake. Lou leaves to get the newspaper and Olive flounders around the kitchen making eggs for the boys with such little finesse I wonder if she has ever prepared a meal in her life. The twins are still in their pajamas; mussed blond tuffs of hair, sleep crust around their eyes. They're telling Sierra a story about Martians and marshmallows, wizards, and blizzards, and I try to follow, but there's no chance.

I ask Olive if I can help her out.

"Sure. Beat some more eggs for me. These kids eat a lot."

I go to work on the scrambling, and she leans against the stove, so close the back of her jeans might catch fire. Again, she has that blurry gaze, like she's both here and living in another city at the same time, with another family.

I decide to go the extra-polite route.

"Thanks again for letting me stay here. I really appreciate it. It's nice to be around a family in a time like this and you have such a lovely home."

She lifts her top lip. I guess it's supposed to be a smile.

"You don't have family?"

"They're in Jersey."

"You don't have friends?"

I rotate the fork so quickly in the bowl that the eggs pull into a perfect open blanket. I move past her to tuck them into the frying pan.

"I just came out of a relationship."

"You're a grown-up when you realize no one's going to take care of you."

"Right."

"Lou is not the cheating type, you know."

I wonder if we're having the same conversation. As far as I can tell, she has no reason to be wary of me, but if there's anything I've learned in my life, it's that I am usually wrong about everything.

"I can tell. He adores you. He talks about you all the time."

"That's right. He does."

And then, "You want some advice, Bean? That's what he calls you, right?"

I nod.

"Guard what's yours."

I don't say anything. Just finish off the eggs while she watches like I'm her employee, the lines of her home clearly drawn.

I eat with the kids. I don't even like eggs but I chew them, slowly, feel them glide down my throat. Lou returns with the paper but puts it away so the kids won't see the pictures or headlines. After I help clean up the breakfast mess, I slip into the living room and pull my bag out from behind the sofa.

I tell them I'm leaving. Thank them too much for their

hospitality. Act like they saved my life but, really, I just want to run.

Lou insists on walking me to the corner. It's all I permit even though he offered to take me all the way back downtown, make sure everything is okay at home. I don't want to look him in the face and I feel bad for that fact. He's been good to me.

"Once it calms down, we can start your lessons again."

I smile, yeah sure. Though I'm obviously out of a job. My workplace doesn't exist anymore. Won't be able to afford those late-night sessions.

He goes for a kiss on my cheek but instead hits the curve between my nose and lip, and I drape an arm around him quick, give him the hug he wants, then pull off and cross the street before the light changes.

On the way home, fellow pedestrians are mute, shock-eyed, and I long for noise. At Union Square, the park is transformed into a shrine lined with candles and posters of the disappeared. I feel inappropriate. We're supposed to be mourning and all I want is to scream.

There he is.

Nico. Sitting on my bed, writing in a notebook. I forgot he still has a key.

"I've been waiting for you," he says.

"How did you know I was coming back?"

"You weren't on the list of the missing. I checked."

He tells me he's been in New York all along. The stint in Los Angeles was brief and pointless and he's been living in Green Point ever since. He walked across the bridge right after the planes hit, made his way to me. Must have arrived right after I left with Lou.

We look at each other a long time. There is no big conversation. No more questions. No push for repentance. For once we're calling it even. I'm here. You're here. That's all we need. In spite of everything, and because love stories never end when they should, I believe we still have a chance.

We tuck into each other like origami, fall asleep like captive hamsters, our lips touching, pretending we're each other's reasons for surviving the cataclysm. We're good for a while, too. Build a pretty pattern of peace—me cooking us dinner, Nico playing with my hair and counting all the ways we're perfect together, starting with the fact that we wear the same size jeans.

I think this is it: the near-death experience we needed to make us work.

For a moment, I'm happy.

It will be months, and most of the wreckage will have already been cleared, before we admit it's not enough. It will be uneventful, the way most life-changing moments are. You don't see them happening.

An April morning. Getting ready for my new job. I will be making my coffee the way I like it: dark, bitter, thick mire with no milk or sugar. He will come up behind me, press his naked chest to my back. He will slip his hand around my mug and take a sip, make a spitting sound and ask how I can drink this shit—say, "Leave it to a Colombiana to ruin the coffee," push me out of the way, "Let me show you how it's done, baby." And I will decide without his knowing, without ever saying, with only an amended gaze that he will never notice, to let the story end.

GREEN

Your mom just called to tell you that Maureen, the girl who tortured you from kindergarten to high school, who single-handedly made it so that you were never welcome in Girl Scouts, soccer, or yearbook, is dead. Maureen, who said you weren't invited to her ninth birthday party because you were too tall and your head would bust through the roof of her house. Maureen, who said that your skin was the color of diarrhea, that your Colombian dad dealt drugs, that boys didn't like you because you looked like their maids, is finally, finally dead.

Officially it was some kind of organ failure, but Maureen is dead because she hasn't eaten in years. You know Maureen went through years of food rehab till her family's money ran out and then she went into the free experimental programs at Columbia Pres. You know Maureen's dad died a few years ago of brain cancer, diagnosed and buried within three months. You know Maureen was a little bananas at the end, because, of all people in the world, she started writing letters to you—not sure how she got your address. You've moved a dozen times since high school, when you had your last blowout with her right after the graduation ceremony. She called you a shit-skinned whore in your white dress, miniature red roses in your French twist. She'd only just started losing weight and you shouted back that she was a fat albino midget no diet would ever save, something you will always regret.

You never knew why Maureen picked you to hate. Her brother was a nice person—made it to Yale and was the family pride. He always asked you how things were going when you ran into him in town. And Maureen's parents were okay people. They even showed up at your grandfather's funeral, said they knew him from the Rotary Club. But Maureen was a monster in a short, tight gymnastics body, thick ankles and black hair from her Portuguese mom, freckled like a dalmatian thanks to her Irish dad.

Your mom is sighing because it's really tragic when a girl you've watched grow up dies.

"And her mother," says your mom. "That poor, poor woman."

She says she'll go to the funeral and maybe you should send the family a card like you did when the interior decorator's son drowned in their pool last summer. You didn't even know the guy but you liked his mom because once, when you were just passing through the living room, she looked up from the upholstery swatches she'd brought your mom to tell you that you had the eyes of a fairy tale.

So Maureen is dead and your mom reads you the obituary they printed in today's paper. Maureen Reilly. Aged twenty-four. Beloved daughter, beloved friend. You remember the Maureen you saw at midnight mass a few years back. Even in heavy winter clothes you could see that her thighs were the size of your wrist. Her eyes bulged and her teeth jutted out of her face like those plastic ones you wind up and let chatter all over the floor for laughs. She'd lost a lot of her hair, got more wrinkles than her mom, the queen of YMCA aerobics. She was just twenty-two or so then, already looked like a corpse and had this stupid look on her face, like she was laughing to a comedy playing in her head.

She saw you and waved from her place on the pew next to her family. You tried not to look at her decaying body, tried to be matter-of-fact about it when your family talked about the sight of her during the car ride home, saying Maureen used to be so cute and look at her now. The only recent gossip you had on her was that her high-school boyfriend, a footballer named Kevin, impregnated and married her former

49

best friend, another ruthless soccer girl named Shannon. You even felt pity for Maureen. You'd just been cheated on for the first time and felt the pain of wounded women everywhere.

A month later, Maureen wrote you a letter. She wanted to get together. She knew you lived in the city now but was hoping you could come out to Jersey. Said she was still living with her parents and was saving up to rent a place in Hoboken or Weehawken. You made the mistake of telling your mom about the letter and she guilted you into going.

You met Maureen at a diner by the train tracks. Ordered yourself a salad and watched her watch you eat it while she ordered herself nothing.

She said, "I'm not sure if you know I've got a problem with food."

You said you had a vague idea. Didn't say it'd been all over the town wires for years already, how she dropped out of some crap college to get treatment, was working a few hours a week gift-wrapping at a local children's clothing store. Not to mention the road map of fat veins that looked like they were trying to break out of her face.

She said, "I remember you did, too. Back in high school. You were so thin."

You don't know how this ended up being about you. Until then, you thought maybe the world was becoming a place of justice and Maureen was looking to repent for her cruelty. But all she really wanted were your diet secrets from the eleventh grade when you decided to carve your soft caramel flesh down to its essence. You went from a cherubic kid to teenage flamingo, one who couldn't go to her tennis lesson without having to endure an hour's worth of comments from the coach about the freakish length of your legs sprouting from your shorts, but no matter how hard you starved, your mushy, unruly breasts refused to shrink. Some girls find pride in their chest but you were ashamed of yours. The concept of a bra embarrassed you and you wore your brother's old sweaters to cover traces of straps. Your mom was always saying a woman should cherish her femininity but you wanted to destroy yours—never wore makeup, always bit your nails and knotted your long hair into a bun.

You overheard two male teachers talking about you once when you sneaked into the teachers' lounge to use the soda machine. Mr. Testa, your AP history teacher, a dork in Dockers who graduated from this very high school ten years earlier, telling the other guy about the black stretch pants with ankle zippers you were wearing that day, how your blue panties showed when you sat at your desk and he circled the room during test time to steal looks, and if there was one girl in the school he'd pay to fuck, it would be you. You felt filthy and when you got home you gave the pants to the housekeeper so she could send them to her daughter in

El Salvador. Even without those pants Mr. Testa offered you a ride home from school several times, asked you to come to his office during lunch hour to talk about your plans for the future. You had a rep for being sort of a nerd even though you also held the cutting-class record for every year that you were in school. But you were a good kid and only skipped class to stay home and read books about women with interesting lives who lived in foreign countries.

One day Mr. Testa invited you to his house to watch a movie and you decided to go to the guidance counselor. Instead of reporting Mr. Testa, you said the class was too hard and you wanted to go back to regular history. You got the worst seat, next to Jerry, the kid who fingered a special-ed girl in the back of the school bus in seventh grade while his friend took pictures. When the teacher wasn't looking, Jerry would mouth dirty things to you and you pretended not to notice.

That was the year of the Great Suicide Epidemic. Not that people were actually dying. There was only one successful case, and it was a parent, not a student. But that death, a pill-popping mom, gave everyone ideas, and soon every Monday at school the halls were filled with talk of who tried to off themselves over the weekend, mostly with prescription pills, vodka, and Tylenol. The latest victim always got a load of attention, until the next weekend when someone else took the spotlight. The theater kids were really into suicide that year. Hardly ever the athletes. And the pudgy unwanted girls with hopeless crushes on popular boys were always a sure thing. The fact is *you* even had a go of it. On your sixteenth birthday. Thirty sleeping pills, but they were herbal, so it wasn't like you were serious about dying either. And nobody noticed anything except that you happened to sleep for a few extra hours.

Your parents are immigrants who don't really understand the concept of depression and who decided to throw you the birthday party of the year, hoping you'd crack a smile. Maureen brought up that party when you saw her that night at the diner, talking like those were the days. The hotel ballroom, the music, the custom-made dress. The only thing you remember about that party is that after the cake, you went out to the parking lot and cried in the bitter January chill because not one person except your brother and cousin asked you to dance. You wished someone would realize you'd fled your own party and come looking for you, but nobody did.

This party was like all the others your parents made you have as a kid, inviting the whole class to your house for magicians and games. At these parties, the parents hung around the living room inspecting your family's furniture while their children were supposed to be playing in the den. But the kids ignored you even though it was your party. The girls came together in little gangs and did cartwheels for one another across the floor. "You try one, Sabina," they'd taunt, knowing full well you couldn't do one. You were always too tall, taller than all the boys even, and you could hardly master your long limbs walking, forget about upside down. The other girls were compact gamines who did round-offs for fun while you were kicked out of Tumble Tots when you were five for your inability to do a proper somersault. The teacher, a frizzy-haired retired professional cheerleader, told your mom you were hopeless and didn't need to come back, even offered to refund her money. Your mom responded in her rich, layered Spanish accent that she and your father weren't planning on selling you to the circus anyway, so there really was no need for you to learn how to roll around on the ground like a potato bug.

The height would come in handy later, much later, when you went to the city with your parents for a Broadway show and had dinner afterward at a nearby restaurant. You went to the bathroom to barf up your meal, and when you came out, a Euro-looking guy in a sharp suit asked if he could talk to your parents, followed you back to your table, and told your dad that you should be a model. Gave them his card and he was a legit guy, one whose name you recognized from fashion magazines. Owned an agency and wanted you to come in for photos. Put his hand on your shoulder and said, "What do you think about that?"

You liked the idea of being beautiful—of being admired without being touched. But you felt like a farce and your dad was quick to insult the man by saying you were meant for better things.

Maureen was wearing a green sweater that day at the diner and for that reason you will always remember her in green. Her once thick hair was a clump of threads tied by red elastic. She wore makeup but on her leathery face it looked clownish and you remember feeling embarrassed to be seen with her. She was talking about when you were kids as though you were best friends.

"Remember in fifth grade when we worked at the goldfish booth at the village fair?"

How could you forget? That was the year Maureen told everyone in class that if they were nice to you, she'd have her dad arrest their parents. And they believed it.

Maureen's dad was a sergeant in town. At one point you thought maybe he or somebody else was touching her and that's why Maureen acquired her armor. Randy, who you befriended in French class, was molested by her stepfather and became a straight-A student who vacuumed her room five times a day. And Nicole, who you knew from horseback riding, had a boyfriend whose uncle raped him his whole life.

"How did you stop?" Maureen wanted to know.

It'd been a long time. You tried to remember.

Your parents got sick of watching you move your food around your plate at dinner, chewing slowly and spitting mouthfuls into a napkin to throw away later, staring at the wall while your dad's eyes watered. Your parents said, How dare you push away your food when the German ancestors you never knew starved to death in a concentration camp, killing an entire branch of your clan, when, for the early days of their marriage, your parents subsisted on sardines and canned beef. How dare you? At the time, the words meant nothing to you. Your mom and dad sent you to a shrink, this incredibly pale English woman who let you call her by her first name. As long as you kept going, your parents kept their hassling to a minimum, paid the shrink bill, and only occasionally bugged you about your diet. You eventually gained a few pounds. Got floppier, fuller boobs. But the discipline to starve was gone.

You gave Maureen all your processed therapy talk. You thought about talking tougher, like your brother did at the height of your famine: No boy will want to kiss your shriveling lips or love your weak body and that chest so sunken that you can almost see your beating heart.

But you held back. Told yourself it wasn't your problem.

Instead you said you had to be on your way, that you had to catch the next train back to the city. Made it sound like you had a really exciting life waiting for you.

Silly to think of it now but before you left each other that day, you still hoped, in that strange space of reminiscing and advice-giving, that Maureen would ask you to forgive her for hurting you, for doing her part to keep you on the town margin. But she only stared at you from across the table with buggy eyes, wrinkled and dehydrated, her flimsy hands shaking as she tried to hold her glass of water.

You told her to write or call you whenever she wanted, said you'd always be there for her if she needed a friend. She hugged you and it felt like air, the mere idea of a hug instead of the real thing even though you could smell the puke on her breath. When another letter did come, you read it quickly, tossed it into the trash, and never thought of Maureen again.

Your plan was to forget. But you did think of her, often, while wishing you could cull your memory to craft a provisional mercy. You never managed. Told yourself, In time. In time.

DESALIENTO

Diego was this guy that I met on Washington Avenue at three in the morning the summer I quit my job at the art gallery and decided I needed a month in Miami to evaluate my next move. Elsa and I had just come out of a nightclub, sweaty, half-drunk, and stinking of cigarettes, because that's how we did it back then. We needed to sober up before driving home, so we went to Gino's for a slice of pizza. Elsa's Ukranian, a magnet for Russian guys, and within seconds she was showing off her Moscow slang to some guy named Vlad who was handing out flyers for the full moon party. Vlad pulled up a chair, and then his friend showed up: a shirtless Argentino—there are millions in South Beach—wearing camouflage shorts and a pair of blue eyes like they were all he needed to get by. He spotted Vlad and dropped his own flyers on our table, sat next to me, and said this is where he needed to be.

You know how it is when you're twenty-three and looking for meaning. I was so empty back then that Diego seemed prescribed by the gods. We gave him and Vlad a lift to Opium because they were supposed to hand out flyers outside the club. They got paid twenty dollars a night for that work. When they got out of our car Diego stuck his head in through my window and kissed me like some kind of satyr, deep, wet, and fast. Before I knew it, he was halfway down the block.

We were staying in my parents' condo. Told everyone we were reflecting on our lives. But really we were just tanning and partying. We made a ton of beaded jewelry and tried to sell it on Ocean Drive but we always ended up giving it away to guys who flirted with us. And when we weren't smoking cigarettes on the beach, we were at Diego's place. He lived in a one-bedroom apartment in the craziest building on Collins, where they rent by the month and the lobby is a revolving stage of drag queens, college kids, hookers, and the men who love them. And then there were the illegals: kids who should be in school or something but they were exiled from wherever they came from by either a shit economy or a miserable home life. Diego shared his apartment with fifteen others. The bedroom had eight mattresses on the floor and they all slept there like it was war times. Most of these kids were from Argentina, like Diego, fleeing last year's collapse; backpackers-turned-refugees working valet parking at the hotels and clubs while the girls waited tables at the cafés on Lincoln where they don't ask for papers.

Vlad lived there, too, and while he and Elsa huddled on the couch talking about how he fled Lithuania by stowing away on a cruise ship and jumping off at New York harbor, Diego and I sat on the balcony smoking and drinking yerba maté from his special gourd. He didn't try to kiss me again after that first night. I was mad for his fat lips and clear eyes, his choppy singsong Spanish and the way he thought shirts were optional. When I complained to Elsa she just rolled her eyes at me and said, "You always do this."

Even when we got sloppy drunk in the pool, beer cans floating next to us, me on his shoulders for a chicken fight trying to knock Elsa off of Vlad, Diego never made a move. Even when we ended up sleeping in the same bed, like that time we all drove down to Key West in nothing but our bathing suits and ended up staying for three days. We washed our swimsuits in the bathroom and let them dry. Vlad and Elsa in one bed doing God knows what, and me and Diego in the other, chaste as virgins.

I knew Diego slept with tons of other girls. There was this one, Valeria, a Uruguayan fox with long black curls, who seemed to own only hot pants and halter tops. She was twenty-six, and I pointed out that she was older than Diego and me every chance I had. She gave him a hundred bucks to buy herself a spot in the aparto/hostel for a couple of weeks, and when we'd all be hanging in the living room, the guys strumming Soda Stereo songs on their guitars, Valeria would dance along like it was her only currency. Diego, like all the other guys, watched her tiny thighs jiggling and the way she was always picking the spandex out of her crack.

There was another one. Roberta the Chilena whose father owned a shoe store in Hialeah and who fell in love with Diego one night at Automatic Slims. I wasn't around, because I was on a real date with some Peruvian UM med-school fool, son of a family friend, and if I didn't go out with him I'd hear about it for a year from my mom. Roberta offered to marry Diego on the spot because she had her papers already. And Diego was considering it, which made me nuts. She said he'd have to work in the shoe store with the family though, and Diego wasn't sold on that last detail. We were at the nude beach one cloudy afternoon when he was thinking it over out loud. I was topless and Diego was completely on display, which, looking back, should have been awkward for us, but it wasn't.

I asked him if he was going to go through with it, trying not to sound jealous.

"I'd rather marry you," he said, and I think he meant it as a joke but it didn't come out sounding that way. Still, I laughed and he laughed, too.

"I'm serious," he said after a minute or two. "If it came down to it, would you marry me so I can get my papers?"

I shook my head. "I'd only marry for love."

"Easy to say when you're not illegal."

Diego didn't believe in love. He read a lot of socialist lit and Osho, and he said love was an imagined condition of the weak. Elsa entertained his debates on the subject while I just turned my eyes to the sky. He said he'd never felt anything in his life that resembled the popular notion of love. Not for anyone except maybe his parents. I took this as a challenge. And when I got him alone one night, sleeping in my bed after another drunken barbecue, I poked him awake with my finger and said, "Diego, I'm going to break your heart one day."

He turned his big eyes on me and said, "I hope you do."

I wish I could say my life changed after that summer but it didn't. I went back to New York and got another shit job in a gallery, this time uptown. Diego and I would talk on the phone a few times a week. He gave up handing out flyers and got a busboy job at one of the big clubs. He came up to the city to see me for a few days and I took him all over: Central Park, Chinatown, the Met, and the Museum of Natural History. He'd never seen a dinosaur and said the bones along with the skyscraper skeleton of New York City made him feel insignificant, like he could just disappear and nobody would notice.

Diego's mom was dying of cancer and he wanted badly to go home and see her but his parents insisted he stay here, that there was nothing left for him in Argentina. No jobs, no opportunity, and if he ever left the United States, he would not be able to come back. We were sitting in my living room, rain pouring outside, turning the city into a giant puddle. He was eating choripán, the only thing he ever ate, and I was drinking a coffee from Abdul the Tanzanian's place downstairs.

"You're my best friend, Sabina."

"I am?"

He nodded, sausage filling his cheek.

I'd go back to Miami when I could, see Diego who was now dealing pot although he didn't want to admit it. He had to, though, when I asked him where he got the money to buy not one but two motorcycles, in addition to an Isuzu Trooper and kite surfing gear. He was rolling in the dough now, sending loads back to his parents, spending some, and saving the rest in a white tube sock in the back of his closet, which he said I should rescue if he ever got arrested.

"How will I know if you've been arrested?" I asked him and he said that he'd use his one phone call to reach me.

It was a cool November night and I'd taken a few days off from work to be there. I went to see him at his new place, a cute townhouse on Euclid with its own patio and everything. His new-arrival cousin Nacho was staying with him. The primo was another knockout, taller and tanner than Diego, with delicate features. He spoke English with a British accent, which Diego thought was ridiculous, and he was always asking me about art, which I liked. But Diego said it was just because Nacho was trying to land himself a rich girl and I felt instantly stupid.

Diego had to go make a delivery, so Nacho and I were alone in his place. Diego had photos up on his wall of our Key West road trip with Elsa and Vlad. I missed Elsa a lot. After that summer, she decided she had had enough of life as a Manhattan financial analyst and went to Russia to teach English, but decided she hated it and went on to Israel to work in a kibbutz. She'd write me that I should go join her there, that working with your hands in a community kitchen is much better than it sounds. She said she was growing out her blonde hair, which, for Elsa, was a big deal. She was talking about getting her Israeli citizenship and I was like,

"Elsa, you're from Jersey," but she said it didn't matter, that she belonged over there now.

Diego had blown up and framed one photo that Elsa or Vlad must have taken of us without our knowing. It was during the drive down, when we pulled over in Key Largo to swim at Pennekamp. We were the only people there and the sea was flat as glass. Diego and I were up to our waists in water and he reached over to hold my hand, just as some dolphins started flipping in the distance. Like a fucking movie scene.

I remember thinking I might be in love with him. But that evening he met some sorority girl in Mallory Square in Key West and sneaked off to be with her. I'd ended up crying on a bench while Elsa and Vlad were inside a bar. Then Elsa came out to hold my shoulders and told me that none of this was real.

"You don't really want him," she said. "You just think you do because he's always there."

Nacho was next to me, handing me a drink, some expensive beer, which was funny because I remembered that when I first met Diego the only beer he bought was Natural Ice, which gave us the worst headaches ever.

Nacho came to South Beach for modeling. Apparently he was already pretty successful at it in Buenos Aires, thought he'd make it big here, but they said he was too old already, almost thirty. "I'm not like my cousin," he kept telling me with distaste, which I thought was a pretty shitty thing to say since his cousin was the one putting him up and giving him dollars to spend. But Nacho thought Diego was from the dirt side of his family and that the fact that he was dealing was shameful, and what's weirder is that I found myself defending him, saying Diego dealt pot with integrity.

"I have a business degree," Nacho told me from across Diego's living room. "I'm an entrepreneur. I have so many ideas. I just need a little backing to start and I'll make a killing. I'm brilliant, you know."

I thought of that old joke you always hear Colombians telling: How do you kill an Argentino? Make him stand on his ego and jump.

I laughed to myself and Nacho looked offended, then shot point blank: "So what's a girl like you doing hanging out with a guy like my cousin?"

"You don't know anything about me or what kind of girl I am."

"I know you're a rich girl who likes to play poor."

It sucks when a perfect asshole manages to hurt your feelings. It was even harder to confront that Nacho was so good-looking and the art history major in me was a martyr for aesthetics, which is why I ended up letting Nacho kiss me on Diego's couch.

To this day I don't know if Diego found out about me and Nacho getting busy like that while he was out. But just a few days later Diego kicked Nacho out, saying Nacho had stolen some cash from him. "I don't care if our mothers are sisters," he said. "Nobody is going to eat my food and then rob me."

The next summer, Elsa was pregnant. She met this Israeli guy in a Tel Aviv nightclub and they fell in instant love. She was living with him in Jerusalem and I thought she was bananas but part of me envied her. I was back in Miami for two weeks, on a date with some other son of a family friend, set up through the Colombian Diaspora dating network. He was a few years older than me, some kind of Brickell banker and he seemed potentially cool, not uptight like the other Colombian guys around. I was always getting set up with these superlame hijos de papi. I rejected all of them, earning me a rep as a failed Colombiana, or possibly a lesbian, and my mom pretended this didn't worry her. After dinner I suggested we go to this club on Miami Avenue, where Diego told me he was going to be. He and I still spoke often, but he had a new girl, his first real novia. He even dared say he loved her a little bit.

He had told me her name was Petra and he had met her at Churchill's. He'd said she was a real rocker chick who rode a skateboard better than Tony Hawk. At the club, my date, Juan Carlos, went to get us drinks while I went looking for Diego. I spotted him shirtless and drunk in the back garden. But before I made it to him for a hug, some short girl with spiky orange hair jumped in front of me, saying, "Stay away from him, he gave me herpes."

Diego laughed it off, introducing his girl Petra and saying that was her trick for keeping other girls away. Later, Petra warmed up and even gave me a brief history of her tattoos, all five of them, from the evil clown on her calf that she got the first time she ran away from home at thirteen to the blue rose on her forearm, in honor of some boyfriend who caused her three abortions. Sure enough, Petra had her skateboard in hand. She also had enough facial pockmarks to play pinball, and Diego looked positively addicted, littering her shoulders with kisses while I introduced Juan Carlos.

"Your friends are nice," Juan Carlos told me when he dropped me off at home later. The guy couldn't wait to get rid of me.

I'm jobless again and came down to Miami for another break at the condo. Diego is right here next to me on the balcony. We're smoking cigarettes and it's been two years since we met, but to me, he's the one who looks older. His formerly taut abs are hiding under just a little bit of mush but he's still without a shirt all day, even when we went for lunch earlier, which would only fly in a place like Miami. Everywhere else, you'd get arrested. But here he's blanco even if he's Latin, which makes him slip under the radar. He's got mad luck and fifty grand stuffed into that same tube sock.

Diego's been trying to break up with Petra for months now but the girl just won't move out, so now he says he's got to be the one to go. He say's he'll leave her with a few months' paid rent so she doesn't have to go back to stripping at the crappy place on Biscayne, put a lump of cash in the freezer for her, and hope she won't spend it on a pair of boobs.

Since I met him, Diego's been threatening to bail on Miami, drive from here to Mexico, then down to the Nicoya Peninsula, and make it a five-year journey back to Argentina. His mom passed away last December and his father is really hurting for money since their pesos turned to paja.

"Are you really leaving?"

"Maybe tomorrow. Maybe the next day. One day you'll call me and I won't be here."

He's always said that when he goes, it will be without a good-bye because what are good-byes good for anyway?

"I'd stay if you married me," he says with the same smile he gave me that pizza night on Washington. The same night he ducked his head into the car and planted one on me.

I can feel it coming and this time I'm ready for it.

Diego disappears the way he said he would, without a word. He calls me from California. He drove that Isuzu all the way there and managed not to get pulled over once. After California it's Mexico and somehow his crossing the border hurts because that's his last step out of here, through the Venus flytrap.

Elsa says she's happy in Jerusalem with her husband, who lays bricks for a living, and her baby, who will speak Hebrew. She says I should come visit and I keep promising her that I will.

"Remember that summer," she says every time I get her on the phone, and then she asks me about Diego, if I've heard from him.

"Not in months," I tell her, but I'm sure he's okay. Diego always gets by.

And just when I've started to forget about him, Diego calls from Playa del Carmen. He's been living in a cottage on the beach, making back plenty of money from a bar he invested part of his savings in. He ran into his cousin in el D.F. Nacho went out there to try to get on one of the Mexican soaps, since they love casting pretty Argentinos.

I catch him up on Elsa and my life though there's not much new to report on my end—only that I recently repainted my bedroom. I've just started dating the Swedish bartender who works at the bar across the street, but I keep that to myself. Diego doesn't say anything and for a second I think the connection has dropped but then I hear him sigh.

"My father died, Sabina. Three months ago. I didn't even know he was sick."

I've had enough people close to me die to know that it doesn't mean anything when people tell you they're sorry. But I say it anyway.

"Now there's really no reason to go back," he tells me. And we both know there's no way for him to come back here unless he's going to try it coyote-style.

"I'm thinking of opening up a little hotel here," he goes on and his voice lifts a little. Typical Diego, not letting anything get him down too long. "A simple place where people can stay by the beach and get high. The hotel that Miami weed built."

"Beautiful." I laugh and then we both get quiet. I imagine him looking out at the sea, like we did that day in the Keys with the dolphins. I'm looking out my window at Fourteenth Street. I can hear that kid playing drums on his plastic bucket on the sidewalk under my window. And then Diego says my name, says it like it's the first time.

"Sabina. You there?"

"I'm here."

"You broke my heart just like you said you would. Like the fucking wind. You broke it wide open."

And because my Diego is no fan of farewells, he just hangs up.

PALOMA

My father thought the aneurysm was going to kill him, and when it didn't, a new era began for our family. He quit his two-packs-a-day Parliament smoking habit. Mami made him promise to cut back his hours at the factory, too—no more working through the weekend. And vacations—before the surgery we hardly took any. But after the doctors opened his skull and clipped out the bubble of trouble, Papi promised Mami that as soon as his hair grew back and the vertigo went away, he'd take her to the Bahamas, where they'd gone on their honeymoon a hundred years earlier.

We had a maid, a Peruvian-Japonesa grouch named Nila who only ever cooked breaded chicken and yellow rice, chased me out of the kitchen with a broom, and said, "Yo no se nada," every time you asked her anything. Lately she was stealing my stuff. A little porcelain unicorn my tío gave me for my first communion. A purple bathing suit I got for Christmas a few years back. Every time I told my mother this she dismissed me and said I was the one who had a habit of losing things. And why would Nila want a unicorn or a little girl's swimsuit anyway? Nila had men calling her all the time, which made no sense because she lived with us, even on weekends, and only ever went out on her own to go to the Pentecostal church in Paterson. Nila couldn't speak English or drive, and since Cristían and I were both still in elementary, there was no other remedy: Tía Paloma had to come and watch over us while our parents were away.

"This is going to be interesting," Cris said when Paloma arrived. She came on the bus that left her by the Grand Union and Papi went to pick her up at the station. She had a week's worth of clothes packed into a small black nylon duffel with brown handles. When she said, "Hola, niños," Cris and I dutifully went over to kiss her before Mami had a chance to tell us we were savages with no manners.

Paloma had no kids and I always got the feeling she was nervous around us. I was nine and Cris was an angry twelve. He'd just decided he didn't want to be a nerd anymore, taken up martial arts, had an arsenal of Chinese stars, butterfly knives, and nunchucks that he threatened me with every time I got too close to his room.

The next day, when Mami and Papi were getting ready to leave for their trip, we stood at the top of the driveway to see them off. Paloma had a hand on each of our shoulders as our parents climbed into the taxi headed for the airport.

"What if they die in the Bahamas, who will take care of us?" I asked Cris as my mother blew kisses from the taxi window. Papi was busy looking over the airline tickets. He never looked back after saying good-bye.

"We'll be orphans," Cris said. "Maybe we can go live with the McAllisters."

The McAllisters were our neighbors. Former Hell's Kitchen Irish folks who invited us over whenever they barbecued—even after my uncle went to the slammer—and the only people who never called animal control when our dog, Manchas, got loose. That's why we liked them.

"They'll be fine. But if anything ever happens, I'll take care of you," Paloma said, reminding us she was our madrina, next in line to our parents.

When the taxi disappeared down the street and we went back in the house, Cris told Paloma that he'd rather eat possums and sleep in the gas station bathroom than live with her. Paloma looked sad for a second then hissed, "Chino malcriado," but Cris was already headed upstairs to his room. It wasn't anything he hadn't heard before.

*   *   *

Paloma was my mother's half sister, older by twelve years.
Her father was a Cuban who died when his plane crashed in
the Amazon when Paloma was seven. Her mother made a
living buying clothes from factories in New York and bringing them back to sell to society ladies in Colombia, while
Paloma went to boarding school in Jamaica and spent her
school vacations in Pereira with her aunt Isabel, the family
lunatic who used to lock her in the closet for hours while
she went out to play cards with her friends.

Paloma's mother, also named Paloma, found a replacement husband quick. He was a Gregory Peck look-alike, a
decorated army general, grandson of a president, and man
of the people, though his biggest selling point was his blue
eyes, so beautiful they made women cry, making it difficult
for him to be faithful. The new marriage produced three more
children—the first, my mother, whom the young Paloma
hated upon conception.

The Paloma I knew lived in a tiny studio apartment
on East Forty-fourth street. The kitchen was the size of
a broom closet and only one person could stand in it at a
time. Same for the bathroom with its cracked claw-foot tub
and missing floor tiles. She slept on a full-size bed pushed
against the wall, and it also served as a sofa when she had

the rare guest. There was an armchair, a wooden trunk that she used as a coffee table, and stacks of books covering every free inch of the apartment—a massive collection Paloma was saving for when she retired. Until then, she mostly did crossword puzzles and word finders, with her bifocals slipping off the tip of her nose. She spent hours at it. And you couldn't turn on the TV when she was at work on one of her puzzles. Noise really bothered Paloma. Mami said Paloma spent so much time alone that she wasn't used to it anymore.

Paloma had enormous breasts, even after two surgical reductions, and wore pointy bras so that her breasts poked out under her loose blouses like they were looking to start a fight. She was heavy but in a way that tells you it came with old age. She still had a thin face, pale, always without makeup, and she kept her brown hair short like a schoolboy, parted on the side with wispy, innocent bangs. She always wore slacks and supportive shoes for walking the city streets, and had the glare of a real lonely New Yorker with a list of complaints about the taxes, the pollution, crime, and the mayor. Paloma had been in New York for thirty years but she spoke English as if she had arrived last week. She recklessly spliced her two languages, but she wrote perfectly in English and was skilled at dictation. Her voice, though, carried more than an accent, constantly cracking as if a thousand years of tears slept under every breath.

Paloma was married once but her husband, a Long Island gringo named Martin, died the day I was born, from a thundering heart attack while smoking a cigarette on the corner of Second Avenue. The next day, my mother's father died.

"You see," my brother would tell me, "you were a curse on our family."

"You're the curse!" I'd snap before Mami would yell at us to stop fighting like gang members.

The truth was that if there was a family curse it was my brother's fault. He was born when our parents were newly-weds working in Puerto Rico, during a year when there was a severe shortage of baby boys born on the island. He was the only barón born in the hospital that week and a nurse tried to steal him—whether it was to keep him for herself or to sell him, we don't know. Paloma spotted the nurse trying to leave the floor with him, ran after her, and snatched baby Cris out of her grasp just in time. A nearby security guard cuffed the nurse, who retaliated with maldición: "A curse on all your family" she screamed, "and never a boy to be born to you or yours again." Three years and a miscarriage later, I was born.

Paloma often reminded Cris that if it weren't for her, he'd be living with some Puerto Rican family in Caguas and certainly not playing video games in New Jersey. This pissed Cris off big-time and I can't say that I blame him because nobody wants to be reminded of the favors they owe. But Cris is also the kind of person who will listen to your secrets with best-friend eyes and then throw them in your face when you least expect it. Like when I confessed to him that I had a thing for our neighbor, Tim McAllister, Cris swore he'd take it to the grave but the next time Tim came over to play Frogger, Cris spilled the beans, and Tim pretty much ignored me after that.

There was a man Paloma considered to be her boyfriend, but my parents didn't like him, so we didn't see him often. He was a tall, white-haired Canadian named Gerald, who my dad said never made a move for the tab if you went out to dinner with him. He often slept over at Paloma's place and they went on vacations together once a year to extremely boring places like Taos and Nova Scotia.

When Paloma came to watch us the week that my parents were in the Bahamas, I thought I would use the opportunity to try to understand her better. We were sitting at the kitchen table. Nila had stepped up the cooking for Paloma's visit, probably because she knew that Paloma wouldn't hesitate to tell my mom if she was slacking. We were eating fish, a rarity in our house. My mother is from the mountains and doesn't feel comfortable eating anything besides a cow. But Paloma said fish was healthier. She'd gone to the Grand Union earlier that day, driving Mami's red Cadillac, and bought the fish herself. It was just the two of us having dinner. Cris stayed to eat at the house of his Taiwanese friend, Joe.

"Why don't you marry Gerald?" I asked Paloma because back then I thought everybody wanted to be married.

"We're happy as friends," she told me, and then asked me if I'd finished my homework.

That was a subject I wanted to avoid. I was only in fifth grade and already an established underachiever. I went to my room. But later, the rest of the story came out.

Cris was late to come home, so Paloma called Joe's house. His mother answered and told Paloma that Cris had not been there that evening. She put Joe on the phone, and after some coaxing, he confessed that Cris was really hanging around with Tania, the local Girl With Problems. He finally showed up a few hours later, high on his experience, whatever it was. When he walked in through the back door of the house, Paloma rushed him, grabbed him from behind the neck, and forced him onto a chair at the kitchen table for an interrogation.

He folded his arms across his chest, raised his chin in the air, and squinted his eyes so much he could probably only see his own arrogance through those lashes.

"You're only twelve and you already want to be some kind of perro puto?" she yelled, and it seemed to me she was taking this very personally. If my mother were here, she'd just tell him not to do it again and keep him moving up to his room. Cris was a perfect student—a free ride through all sorts of bad behavior as long as he kept delivering As.

Cris grinned, his silver braces catching the light and making stars on the ceiling.

"Don't you laugh at me," Paloma snarled.

"You're not one to judge," Cris ripped. I could tell he'd been saving this one.

"What does that mean?"

"Don't call me perro puto when you're just a mistress. Got it?"

I wasn't sure what a mistress was but I knew it was bad, maybe as bad as a puta pagada, which is what my parents called the women my uncles sometimes hung around with instead of their wives. Paloma was stunned and Cris used the window of shock to make his escape and retreat to his room. All we heard was the door slam. Paloma was frozen, one hand on the kitchen table as if her body was laying down roots.

"Are you okay?" I asked her. Nila had already gone to bed. I was glad she wasn't there to see the show. I offered Paloma a glass of water. Told her maybe we could make some tea. But she just shook her head, and finally I told her good night.

* * *

Paloma left her job keeping the books at Panasonic and went to work at the Museum of Modern Art, which made her happy because she could get all kinds of discounts on stationery and tote bags from the gift shop. My mom often went to meet her for lunch and a walk around the museum while my brother and I were at school and Papi was at work. My mother didn't have many friends, but that never struck me as weird because my father didn't have many either, just a ton of siblings who kept marrying, divorcing, and multiplying, so there were always a lot of people around anyway.

Mami was on her own in the United States, if you didn't count her husband or kids. She left her parents behind in Colombia and they both died before I had a chance to meet them. She had a few siblings left in Bogotá: one full sister, one full brother who was institutionalized for retardation, and another half sister that her father had with a secretary. Around here, Mami only had Paloma, and they clung together like schoolgirls, linking elbows as they walked, talking for hours about people I didn't know, about the world they left behind in South America, in a way that made it sound like a miniseries.

You could hardly tell they were related though. Paloma with her bare face next to Mami's hour's worth of cosmetics, perfectly layered creams and pigments, so that her eyes seemed lit from within. My mother always dressed as if she were on her way to a cocktail party, while Paloma had on her sensible uniform—black trousers and a blouse in one of the primary colors. My mother had the soft, forgiving nature of a mother, infinite patience unless you crossed her, and then she became a viper. Paloma seemed infinitely wounded, trusted no one, never accepted when you tried to give her a gift, and always wore her purse across her chest with a hand clutching the strap, prepared to be mugged.

Paloma was happy working at the museum until a shiny Colombian compatriota named Oscar showed up, with oily hair that looked like it might drip on you if you got too close and a face that always looked wet. I saw this wonder myself one day when I went with my mother to meet Paloma at the museum. Oscar was always talking about the various women he was screwing, going into detail at the dirty parts so as to annoy Paloma, whose desk was next to his in accounting. And then his harassment became outright cruel. He'd call her fat, grotesque, mock her, told her he was going to have her fired with the false complaints he filed against her in personnel on a weekly basis. Paloma didn't know what to do but she was tough, so she ignored the man, who was slowly poaching the few friends she'd made on the job. She had only one left. A recent college grad named Maggie, who had the kind of red hair you only see in movies. I think Maggie had a sad family story of her own and that's why she gravitated toward Paloma.

When Paloma came to our house in New Jersey to spend the weekend, she would tell me about her. "Maggie is so sweet, she buys me a bagel and coffee every morning without my asking her to." Or, "Maggie has to buy a dress for a party and she asked me to go shopping at Macy's with her."

I got the feeling she was comparing me to Maggie. At that time I was fifteen and had an especially sucky attitude. When Paloma invaded the family room, sleeping on the couch so that I couldn't watch television when I wanted, I took to ignoring her, isolating her with my indifference. My mother never pushed us to be close with each other. Our distance seemed to reinforce her own conflicted past with her sister and every now and then she'd fall into a memory and say, "Paloma used to be terrible to me," before she stopped herself, shook out her hands as if they were full of crumbs, and added, "Well, never mind. That's all in the past now."

At that time, our maid was a young Guatemalan lady with a mouth full of gold. Her name was Deisy and she'd buy turtle eggs from some store in North Bergen and eat them for lunch right there on our kitchen table. I told her they were endangered but she'd just say they were delicious, peeling away the soft shell to reveal the turtle fetus; tiny head with eyes closed and claws tucked inward. Deisy had only recently arrived but she was picking up English quickly from talk radio, and my father gave her a list of vocabulary words every morning that she'd memorize by the evening. It was Deisy who told me I needed to start treating Paloma better.

I confessed that I didn't feel any warmth toward Paloma, no matter if she was my aunt or my godmother.

Deisy shook her head at me and said, "Ser amable no quita lo valiente."

We made a deal. She'd give up eating turtle eggs and I'd be nicer to Paloma.

Holidays in our home consisted of my mother hosting all of my father's family. Paloma came, too. She'd help my mother organize the food, set up the table, supervise the housekeeper so that everything was perfect. But then, as the music and chatter filled the house and the relatives fell into their pods of conversation, Paloma was always left alone on the sofa. People avoided her, maybe because they didn't quite know what to say. You couldn't ask her about her boyfriend because by now everyone knew he was married to another woman in Parsippany and that he was probably never going to leave her despite his stringing Paloma along all these years. You couldn't ask her about her job at the museum because then you'd have to hear about Oscar El Demonio for an hour, how he was trying to push her out of her job, force her to quit out of frustration, but she refused to give him the pleasure.

Or she'd talk about all the things she was going to do in a few years when she retired. She had all these trips in mind: Southeast Asia, Russia, Brazil, and South Africa. She even wanted to go back to Jamaica to see the Kingston boarding school where the nuns tormented her, the place where she first understood what it meant to be alone and possibly forgotten. And of course, as soon as she retired, she would finally start reading all the books that formed a fortress around her apartment.

But these conversations hardly ever happened because people didn't give her the chance. Only my mother. When Mami was done feeding the people and taking compliments on the food and party, she'd go straight over to Paloma, and the two would fall into their song of history, exchange glances packed with gossip and innuendo about the other guests, which only the two of them could understand.

My mother's mother died of cancer. Mami said it was because her husband's infidelities had already demolished her that she handed herself over to the disease. She didn't undergo any treatments and refused to go to the hospital. She stayed in her own bed, her body shrinking into the same sheets she'd embroidered for her wedding, while her absent husband returned home from the apartment he now shared with a mistress, to be with his wife during her last days.

Mami says that during that last month, when she left my brother and father behind to go home to Colombia, is when she really got to know her mother. All the daughters spent hours in bed with their mother, told stories, rubbed lotion on their mother's legs and skin until she said that the pain was too great, her flesh burning from the inside out. For her last days, my mother says that her father became the perfect husband. There was no mention of his mistress or the child he'd had with her. As he sat at his wife's bedside, he told her she was the love of his life, asked her to forgive him, and said there was no other woman that compared to her in beauty and in spirit. Mami said the worst part was that she could see in her mother's eyes that she didn't believe him. And he wasn't forgiven.

When their mother died, Mami returned to Puerto Rico but Paloma stayed in Colombia for a while. My mother says they were not close then, but she heard from others that Paloma became addicted to sedatives, fell into an enormous depression, and that she spent months crying into the pillows of her mother's bed.

*　　*　　*

It was no surprise then when Paloma was diagnosed with cancer. Her mother's had appeared in the pancreas, lethal, the kind of cancer that seems to take pleasure in the killing. Paloma's cancer revealed itself in her uterus. More than one doctor told her it was because she'd never had children, as if she were to blame.

I was twenty, at college in Manhattan, when my mother told me. I was impatient and asked her flat out if this meant Paloma was going to die.

"It's not like in the old days," Mami told me. "They say they caught it early and she'll go right into chemo. She should be fine."

Paloma lost her hair. At first she wore a scarf around her head or one of her old hats left over from the seventies. She lost a ton of weight with the treatment; her cheeks sank and her eyes bulged, while her lips became floppy. Her large breasts began to sag even farther and she held a constant expression of terror. Mami said we should be extra nice to Paloma, so I tried calling her every week to see how she was feeling. She was still working despite her fatigue and treatment schedule, never mind the nausea and depression that followed each session. She was still holding out for her retirement, her pension, saying once she kicked this cancer and got that cash in her pocket, she was going on a world tour.

My mother went with her to the doctor sometimes. It was on one of those visits that a new doctor who was seeing her for the first time asked her if she'd ever had children. She said no, but the doctor went further and asked if she'd ever been pregnant.

"Four times," Paloma answered while my mother lost her breath.

"And what happened?" asked the doctor.

"I lost them."

Nobody knew Paloma had ever been pregnant. She never told my mother. My mother asked her why she'd kept it a secret all those years but Paloma didn't have an answer.

My parents convinced Paloma to take a vacation when her treatments were finally over. Paloma hardly ever took vacations, especially in the spring, because she said that they needed her at the museum during tax season. Papi always said Paloma did the work of a dozen people. But Oscar was still abusing her on the job, making fun of her bald head, telling her she looked like a hairless monster.

We went to Israel. The Holy Land.

At the time, I was dating a Lower East Side Costa Rican named Roly so I was too busy missing him and hoping he wouldn't cheat while I was away to appreciate that we were walking in the footsteps of Jesus. Paloma's hair was growing in, a dark fuzz much curlier than expected. Her face reclaimed some of its pink and she seemed invigorated by the dust and stone of Jerusalem. Paloma never went to church in New York, probably still mad at the nuns in Jamaica, but in Israel, I saw her fall into silent meditation at those holy sights packed with tourists, waiting in line behind dozens of people just for the chance to kneel before the Holy Sepulchre.

We went to the Jordan River where there was a troop of born-agains baptizing themselves. The tour guide said the water was holy, so Paloma pulled out an empty Evian bottle and filled it up with the river water. I think she planned to anoint herself with it to keep away the cancer but I didn't ask specifics. Some things are just personal.

Mami later said to me, "I think this trip is a new beginning for her. She says she's not going to work so much from now on. She might even retire early."

But when we got back to the States, it was business as usual. Paloma returned to her life at the museum, her nights with Gerald, and the occasional weekend at our house in New Jersey. Sometimes I called her to say hi even though it felt unnatural to me, just to make my mother happy. Paloma hardly seemed interested in talking to me, though, and gave the same monotone replies that I'd once offered as a snotty fifteen-year-old. I felt insulted. I wanted to ask her, "What did I ever do to you?" but I knew the answer. Nothing.

They said if the cancer stayed away for five years, Paloma would be in the clear. It came back after two years. This time with full force, having deposited little nodules in her lungs, so firm in the tissue that there was no way to retrieve them. She went in for another round of radiation and chemo. She had to take time off from work and my mother brought her to stay at our house because the doctor said Paloma's studio was too dusty for her lungs. Mami took her there to pack up some things and I think both of them knew it would be the last time.

My mom asked me to come home to Jersey to spend some time. My brother even made an appearance. Paloma was camped out in the family room, had an oxygen tank beside her, just in case, and she banished the elderly Manchas from sight because she said his fur got into her throat. She would have been more comfortable in one of the upstairs bedrooms but she was too weak to climb the steps without turning purple from exertion.

Our maid at the time was a former nurse who came to the States after her husband was murdered in Medellín. Her name was Luz and I loved her. She had two daughters, who went to work as nannies in Barcelona, and she missed them so much that she sort of used me as a stand-in, making a fresh batch of arepas and lentejas every time I came home, always leaving a steaming cup of cinammon tea on the nightstand before I went to bed. Because she'd been a nurse, Luz was extra good with Paloma. That is, until Paloma started barking at her, telling her she wasn't cleaning well enough because the dust was causing her to cough uncontrollably. Luz almost quit a few times, told Mami she was not used to this kind of treatment, but Mami begged her to stay, finally admitting that the doctors had told her Paloma wouldn't last much longer.

Several times a week, Mami drove Paloma to the city to see her doctors. Every weekend that I came home, I found Paloma more dependent on the oxygen tank, with plastic tubes up her nose and eyes wide as if in the midst of a duel. We kept the house quiet. Paloma couldn't take any kind of noise, which meant that Luz couldn't play her salsa music while she worked in the kitchen, and Mami had to whisper when she spoke on the phone to her other sister in Colombia. Paloma wouldn't even come to the table for dinner. She was losing her appetite. It took all her will to swallow a few crackers and some soup.

All her life, Paloma loved to read the *New York Post.* Never the *Times.* When she was at the house, Papi went out every morning to get her a copy. One day, Paloma stopped reading. Each day thereafter the editions piled up on the coffee table in the family room untouched. My father tried to entice her with the latest news about the mayor or whatever political scandal was in the headlines—all to inspire a little passion in Paloma, but she wasn't interested anymore, and soon she lost track of the days.

Gerald came to see her sometimes. My mother tried to be polite, even asked Luz to make him lunch, coffee, whatever the guy wanted as he sat in the armchair next to Paloma, who didn't even change out of her nightgown anymore. She spent her afternoons on the sofa with her crossword puzzles, and when Gerald came to visit, they sat in silence across from each other in the family room. Sometimes Luz and I hung around the doorway trying to hear the way they spoke to each other but they didn't give anything away. Luz said she could see in Gerald's eyes that for him, Paloma wasn't dying fast enough.

When Paloma was hospitalized, my mother asked me to call her sister in Colombia to tell her to come because there wasn't much time left. Carmen arrived the next day. Papi picked her up at the airport and brought her straight to the hospital. Carmen was two years younger than my mother and they could pass for twins, though Carmen had abandoned the Andean vanity that sustained my mother, in favor of a more European look, wore mostly black and only foundation, which Mami always told her was the wrong shade. Mami warned Carmen not to cry at the sight of Paloma but when she stood at the foot of the hospital bed, the room dimly lit because too much light bothered Paloma's eyes, Carmen folded. Paloma peeled the oxygen mask from her face when she saw her little sister for the first time in over ten years.

"I must really be dying if you're here."

My mother and Carmen slept at the hospital with Paloma, who was increasingly anxious that she would suffocate, her lungs locked with disease. She sucked air from the plastic nasal tubes, ravenous, and called the nurses often, telling them the oxygen tank was broken, not enough air was coming out.

After three weeks, the insurance wouldn't pay for her hospital stay any longer and the doctor told my mother that bringing Paloma back home with her would be a mistake. Mami argued that she could take care of her, with Luz's help, and she would hire a full-time nurse, but the doctor kept shaking his head, and finally took Mami's wrist in his hand and said, "Trust me, you don't want to do this."

I could see what he meant, so it was up to me to spell it out for my mother, tell her that Paloma would die on our sofa. She needed better medical care in case there was an emergency. Mami relented. A few hours later, an ambulance came to take Paloma to a hospice in the Bronx. Mami and I followed the ambulance in her car. I could see my mother was exhausted. She'd been forsaking her makeup and wearing the same black pants and gray sweater for days. Her hair was pulled into a ponytail and she had a folder full of documents with her: Paloma's papers indicating her wishes not to be revived or sustained on machines, leaving my mother to make all decisions on her behalf.

I thought a hospice was a hospital but I learned this is where people come to die. Shriveling bodies in wheelchairs lining the halls, forgotten people waiting for their last breath. As Paloma was set up in her new room, a counselor and a doctor took my mother and me aside to tell us about the different support groups they offer for families of patients.

Mami wouldn't ask, so I took over.

"How long does she have?"

"I would be surprised if she lasts a week," the doctor said, and the counselor woman put her hand on my shoulder. I hate when people you don't know try to offer you comfort. I think she must have sensed this because the hand lasted only a second there before she removed it.

We went to see Paloma in her room, told her she should get some rest. I offered to put on the TV but she said no, that the sound and light bothered her. Her voice was just a whisper now. It took all her might to make out a few words and then she'd quickly put the oxygen mask back on and close her eyes as she drew in her breath. While we were there, she had the oxygen tank changed three times, saying each one was defective.

"They're trying to kill me," she told my mother with panicked eyes.

Mami soothed her, tried to read her some psalms but Paloma didn't want to hear it. She looked at Mami, took the mask off her face, and said, "Go home, Maria. You look terrible."

We each kissed Paloma good-bye. She didn't meet my eyes when I told her I loved her. When I left her room, I spotted a copy of the *Post* on the counter of the nurses' station, picked it up, and brought it back to Paloma's room while my mother continued down the corridor.

I got as close to Paloma as I could, touched her hand as I held the paper in front of her. "Look, Paloma, I found the paper. You want me to leave it here for you?"

She shook her head, pulled her hand out of mine, and waved me away. I told her I loved her again but I don't think she heard me. When I left her, she was fumbling with the oxygen mask again, fighting for each abbreviated breath.

CIELITO LINDO

This morning after you left I stayed in bed a long time trying to find the moment when we both knew what was happening. We were on the sofa leaning on each other, watching *The Godfather*. You ran your fingers all over my arms and I pretended I didn't feel anything. You pulled my face to yours and tried to kiss me and I shook my head and said, "You're not my boyfriend anymore."

You kissed me anyway and I pulled away. My hand brushed against you and I felt you hard and said, "What are you going to do with that?"

"You know . . ."

And I told you to show me.

When it was all over, we lay tangled in the darkness of my bedroom. I almost forgot what year it is but then you started to slide out from under me, pushing the sheets off you, stepping into your jeans, and pulling your shirt on over your head. You leaned over the bed, kissing my forehead while I avoided your eyes and stared out the window.

"Look at me," you said.

I gave you a little smile so you would feel absolved. You kissed each of my eyelids the way my mother used to do when I was a child and disappeared out the door.

The last time we were together like this was eight months ago, Valentine's Eve. The next day, you were distant and I hated that you looked at me with a guilty face. I saw you were ready to blame me for seducing you, as if it would lessen the charge and you'd only face time for second-degree cheating. I wondered if you ever felt that guilty when it was me you were cheating on, with her.

My friend Michael took me to a bar on Washington and while he got wrecked with some strangers, I drifted into the back of the place to play pool with some model boys who are too pretty for their own good. Michael said this was the best night of the year to meet someone new because all the couples are in restaurants and only single people are in the bars. He was right. I looked around and saw that everyone in the place had that same lonely, hungry look in their eyes, like stray dogs looking for owners.

The set just seemed to roll onto the stage and next thing you know I was in this silly boy-meets-girl scene. He asked me to be his partner for the next game. He had his quarters on the pool table for an hour already. I said no, that I just wanted to sit and smoke and I could tell he was a little disgusted watching me light up but he kept grinning at me anyway.

He was really sporty-looking, Star. The opposite of you. He was wearing neat jeans, not soft with two weeks of dirt on them like yours, a button-down shirt, and he looked like the cleanest guy in the bar, out of place, and definitely older than the rest of us. He was so blond, or maybe he just looked like a ray of sun because I'm so used to your black mane. He has fat lips that are split from surfing accidents, a wide nose with a broken bridge, and his skin is tan and cracked with sun damage. He's got a swimmer's body. Huge shoulders, a thin waist. I studied him while I smoked. I sniffed him out the way I sniffed you out. Like the night you and I met at the concert and I knew this was going to be the beginning of something huge in my world. With this guy at the bar on Valentine's, I hoped I would find a distraction for a while, from you.

Lucas wants to know if I'm feeling better today.

"Yeah," I tell him, confident in my lie. "I took some aspirin and went to bed early."

"I called you at least five times last night."

"I know. I heard your messages this morning."

We're in his flashy car. A total midlife-crisis car. He's forty, rich, and single, so he drives a bullet-colored Ferrari. When we stop at red lights, people in the cars next to us always check us out. It's such a stupid car. It makes me think of people starving in third-world countries. I feel guilty riding in this car, and it has nothing to do with the fact that I don't love him.

You never talk about her. I never ask. It's as if she doesn't exist. I'm different. I can't say three sentences without muttering something about "my boyfriend." I know you don't like to hear about him; you've told me so a hundred times. You don't like to imagine that I kiss anyone else. But I can't edit him out like you do so well.

I'm not going to lie. Sometimes I wonder why I even bother running around with you, letting myself become la otra, doing things I swore I'd never do. I tell myself it's okay when you do these things for love. And the other part of me, the sinister self I never knew I possessed, is satisfied to know that at the very least, you're not faithful to her either.

I broke up with Lucas after two months together.

I said to him, "I think we should break up before you get too attached to me."

He started to laugh, showing me all his teeth.

"I'm already attached to you," he said.

"Well, we'd better break up before you fall in love with me."

"I'm already in love with you."

It lasted only two days. I made this case about how we're at different stages in life. He's divorced and has had like fifteen live-in girlfriends. That's all he wants, a professional girlfriend to complement his lifestyle.

He's always telling me how life is about taking pleasure in the day-to-day stuff like surfing, sports, good restaurants, and vacations in Rio and Gstaad, not having a nuclear family on an already overpopulated planet. We have so little in common it's scary. The only thing that keeps him interested in me is his taste for my body.

I can't wear high heels with him though. He's shorter than me and he hates if I extend myself another few inches. Not like you, rising almost half a foot over me. I could wear my highest heels and you'd love it. And, back then, you loved it when I took off everything except those high heels and walked around for you before you'd grab me and throw me on the bed.

Not my boyfriend. In his apartment, you take off your shoes at the door.

But Lucas is devoted. I'm lucky that his age has allowed

him to get any cheater ways he might have had out of his system.

"Promise you won't leave me," he says at the most random moments, like when I'm putting on my makeup to go out for dinner.

"I promise," I always answer, because I don't have the energy for truth anymore.

You've poisoned me, Star, sabotaged me in every way. I was the most faithful girl in the world until I met you, and now we are the same.

It's midnight. We're lying on a blanket on the beach, drunk on red wine and laughing at all the stars in the sky. You lay me on my belly and trace the paths between all the beauty marks on my back, the ones that look like they were made with a Sharpie. You call them my constellations. And the biggest mark, right in the middle of my left shoulder blade, is the brightest star. And the brightest star, I say, is you.

You go on singing me that old song, "Cielito Lindo," and I close my eyes while you whisper the lyrics into my ear. "Ese lunar que tienes, cielito lindo, junto a la boca, no se lo des a nadie, cielito lindo, que a mí me toca . . ."

It just so happens that your girl and my man are both in New York, where you and I met so many years ago. This is just about the funniest thing we can think of right now and we are laughing so hard I feel like my ribs are going to split like wishbones.

"You know what would be really funny," I say, gasping for air, "if we took out my boyfriend's Ferrari."

I can't remember how we got here. Yet somehow we're inching into Lucas's apartment with the key he gave me. You're surveying the whole monstrous place and his slick minimalist furniture while I go to his bedroom and pull his spare set of car keys from the nightstand drawer. When I turn around, you're standing close behind me. You hold onto my hips to keep me from tripping over and falling backward onto the bed.

You're driving the Ferrari fast down the causeway. We fly past palm trees and the Brickell Avenue mirrored high-rises flickering like razors in the moonlight. You drive like it's your car, looking over at me sitting next to you every few seconds, running your fingers through my hair, putting your hand on my thigh, leaning over to kiss me at every traffic light. I'm so happy I almost wish we would crash and die like this, together.

I've only given you one side of the story. The fact is that I'm not really that miserable with Lucas. He's good to me, Star.

He calls me all the time and I always know where he is. He's not a disappearing act like you are. No way would he shut off his cell phone for hours like you used to do. I like the security more than I thought I would. I also like that for once I don't have to be the relationship tutor. He's expressive. He never holds back. Not like you. Getting you to say what you feel is like walking out into the desert and asking God for a sign.

That's why I never told you I loved you either. Not until we'd spent the night together for the hundredth time as cheaters and I decided to lay it on the line right there in the mess of my bed sheets. Remember?

I told you, "If I could, I would reach into my chest, rip out my heart, and hand it to you."

You just stared back at me with your gypsy eyes.

Maybe that's when I let go of the pretty picture I wanted our love to be and accepted the story as it was dealt. Our love isn't dainty colors and perfect proportions set in a neat frame. Our love is more like the graffiti on the walls downtown that they try to wash away and paint over but it's always underneath. Even after a fresh coat of paint someone always creeps up in the night and sprays on some more.

Having an affair isn't that hard. Once you get used to the lying it's all pretty simple. All you need is a probable alibi.

But today Lucas is looking at me like I'm in trouble. He's got something serious to say and he won't spit it out. We're sitting face-to-face on his bed because this is where we always sit, cross-legged, when we're about to have a serious conversation.

"Baby, you know I don't mind you driving the Ferrari while I'm away," he begins.

How does he know? We were so careful. Nobody saw us leave his condo or come back with it. We only added a few miles.

"You left the seat back and it took me forever to return it to the position I like."

He says this like I committed a felony.

I use your recipe for lying. I meet his gaze. I keep quiet and try to look as childlike as possible, sitting still with my lips soft. Silence implies innocence. Only idiots confess. I learned that from you.

It was bound to happen. We're both at the same bar, you with your girl, me with my man. I'm sitting on a sofa along the wall, smoking, while Lucas pretends it doesn't bother him. I'm out of cigarettes and feeling bold, so I make my way to the ladies' room to buy a fresh pack from the bathroom attendant, knowing I'll pass through your line of sight on the way.

As I slice through the crowd on the way back to Lucas, I feel a hand close around my wrist. I look and see you there beside me.

I mouth the words, "Let me go," and you do.

I feel strange to be so near you in a public place. I'm so used to our stolen privacies. My eyes come into focus and I see that she is next to you. I have never seen her before but I know it's her by the way her finger hangs on one of the belt loops of your jeans.

Now it's a game of eyes.

I learned from my mother, the retired beauty queen, that how well a woman speaks with her eyes is what separates the amateurs from the pros. I look at your girl and then at you, feeling your eyes anchor on me as I slip into the crowd.

If she didn't already know we're sleeping together, she does now.

We're in the Ferrari again. It's our little routine, stealing Lucas's car every chance we get. You're speeding and I know it's only a matter of time before we're stopped by the police.

You pull over on the beach along the bay. We put the seats all the way back and for a second I think that maybe you brought me here to tell me you love me. But then you begin to kiss me, ripping into my lips with urgency, pulling the clothes off both our bodies with a famished fury that makes me think this might be the last time.

VIDA

She told me her real name was Davida, that she was named for four men who came before her in her family and that her older brother escaped the tradition because he was a diseased baby who Saint Anthony saved, so his name is Tony. She said she couldn't remember who started calling her Vida but that it happened here in Miami. In Colombia she was never called anything but her given name, but over here Vida stuck, which she said was okay with her because that plane ride over the Caribbean broke her life in two.

I met her at my boyfriend's house, a small pink stucco cube in El Portal. He's Hungarian and has a cluster of compatriots that get together at his place for weekly barbecues in the backyard. I was one of the newer girlfriends and Vida had been with her guy, Sacha, for at least a year or two. But when she showed up she always had those same skittish eyes, like a stray cat who knows it's about to be chased off. She hardly spoke to anyone. It was her man who did the talking with a fixed hand on Vida's waist, and you'd almost think she was his prisoner if it wasn't for the way she always dipped her mouth into the curve of his neck and marked him with kisses. Sacha never broke away from her except to hover around the grill with the other Hungarians, poke the steaks, and talk in their language about the old days in Veszprém.

I didn't mind those barbecues. The boyfriend and I were doing well at the six-month mark, and I had beaten out the other two girls he was sleeping with when I met him: a Mexican and a Nicaraguan. Didn't take a genius to see that the boyfriend and his friends had a thing for girls with a tan but I didn't care. I'd been living in Florida for three years already and only had a few ex-boyfriends to show for it. No female friends, and a community college teaching job that always left me fearing for the future of our youth.

Vida raised an eyebrow at me the first time she heard I was Colombian. The boyfriend said it when he introduced us, as if that's all we needed to become like sisters. I had to clarify that I was U.S.-born, it was my parents who were true Colombians, and Vida accepted that, even appreciated that I took the time to authenticate myself to her. She found my Spanish amusing. Said I talked like it was the seventies. That's the Spanish my parents left with, I told her, the Spanish I learned in our house mixed with the telenovela talk I picked up on Telemundo. The other girlfriends, a Russian girl named Irina and two Hungarian sisters named Valeska and Zora, mostly kept to themselves. That left Vida and me to take refuge in each other during those long afternoons around the picnic table.

Vida didn't work officially. I knew she was illegal like my boyfriend, most of his friends, and about half of Miami. She was pretty: lean with high hips, dollar green eyes, and bouncy black hair. I didn't see why she couldn't get a job in a restaurant or a store. She told me she cleaned houses sometimes, even offered to clean mine for cheap. She said she did makeup nice, too, and if I had a party to go to I should give her a call. I asked her where she learned and she got a faraway look in her eyes and said, "I used to do pageants."

I told her my mom was a beauty queen in her former life. She was a plain Bogotá nerd till some guy pulled her off the street and into a pageant and she ended up a Miss Colombia finalist. The following year, she married my father and moved to Queens and later to New Jersey, where she traded in her tacones altos for driving shoes. Vida seemed to be doing me the favor of listening and when I was through she only asked me where New Jersey was in relation to Florida.

One day, Vida moved past the usual light talk about the weather and food and asked me flat out what I was doing with my boyfriend.

"I don't see you with him," she said with such authority that I felt childish, which was absurd since I was five years older.

"I just like him," I told her, which was true. The boyfriend and I met at the gym where he worked out aging divorcees, sometimes sleeping with them to lift their spirits. He admitted that to me on our first date. We didn't have much else in common—that was no secret. And logistically it wasn't ideal because the boyfriend was in a green-card marriage to a Cuban girl that cost him ten thousand, of which he still owed five.

He was a boyfriend for the shadows, somebody my parents didn't know existed. A boyfriend I spent nearly every night with but with whom I didn't envision any other life. He drove me to the doctor when I had the flu. Took me to the movies and let me pick them. Once I found a text message on his phone from a woman named Claudine, inviting him over for a Parisian lunchtime superfuck, and something in me split, though I never mentioned it.

Vida asked me if I still believed in love. Asked me as if it was something like Papá Noel or El Coco, an imaginary creature sent to taunt us as kids and inspire fantasies. I shook my head and it hurt my heart a little to do so.

"Me neither," she said with a pride that I wanted for myself.

* * *

The boyfriend worked days at the gym but ran a little side business at night as a private driver. When they wanted to get fucked-up on South Beach, the clients called and he'd drive them around in their own car. The boyfriend and Sacha were partners and they rotated jobs, but on some nights they'd both get stuck working. On one such night the boyfriend suggested I hang out with Vida. Told me she was lonely, had no friends, and couldn't drive herself anywhere. I picked her up at her apartment complex, which I'd never been to because she and Sacha always met us when we went out together.

The apartment was a shoddy place on upper Collins near the banged-up motels and right off of drug dealer's row. She was sitting on the front steps smoking a cigarette when I drove up, her hair pulled into a ponytail, wearing jeans and a pink blouse. Almost looking like a private school girl who got lost in the wrong neighborhood.

I thought we'd go for a drink or maybe get dinner, but Vida only wanted to go to the beach, even started begging me to take her there like I was her mother or something. We bought some medianoches at a little Cuban place and parked just before Haulover Beach. Though clouds covered the moon and the shore was dim with night, Vida pulled off her sandals and ran toward the water, went in up to her knees and splashed around in the foam. I sat on the sand and watched her lose herself, shouting things at the clouds.

When she came back to my side on the sand, she ripped into her sandwich and told me she still couldn't grasp the immensity of the ocean, that until last year she'd only seen it on film and on the plane ride over.

"I thought you've been here for years already," I told her. Which was true. She'd told me she came to Miami at twenty-one and I knew she was already twenty-three.

"That's true," she said, rubbing the sand off her ankles with her free hand. "But they didn't let me out of the house the first year."

"What house?"

"Where I was working."

I imagined a horrible employer. A family who hired her as a muchacha. I saw tons of young girls in white maid's uniforms all over Miami, pushing strollers at the park and grocery carts at the supermarket. Maybe she had a boss who locked her away. I'd heard of that. My mom's muchacha was full of terror stories.

Vida faced me but all I saw was the outline of her hair and the car lights flashing in the distance behind her.

"Una casa de sitas."

If my second-generation Spanish was correct, she said a brothel. A place where they take appointments with women. I didn't know how else to say it, so I asked her as plainly as I could what she was doing there. And just like that she said they'd made her a puta.

She pulled her hair out of its tie and wrapped it back up again.

"You think differently of me now, don't you, Sabina?"

"No, of course not."

"I was a nice girl once. Nice family. Everything."

There were so many things I wanted to ask her. Did her family know? Did Sacha know? How did she end up in there and how did she get out? How long did she stay?

"I'm so sorry," I said, like an idiot.

We started talking about other things. She told me that Sacha agreed to pay for her to go to beauty school to learn how to do hair and nails and that he knew a Polish lady in Aventura who would give her a job off the books. Her eyes shone as she told me that her dream was to open her own salon one day.

On the walk back to my car she told me it was her hairdresser who brought her over to Miami. A transvestite named Fito who always did her hair and makeup for the beauty pageants gratis because he said Vida was the best investment in her town, Usme. He told her family he had contacts in Miami and would get Vida auditions at all the Spanish networks so she could be a presentadora on Sábado Gigante or something.

"And your parents let you go?" I was so used to the overprotective pair I'd been dealt, unable to imagine how they could just send her off.

"Oh, my mother had me drinking water from the Flower of Jerusalem. It was supposed to bless me and send me on a journey, so when Fito offered to pay for my ticket, Mami thought it was the work of God."

I had to ask. Flower of Jerusalem?

"She kept it in a glass bowl next to the television and we had to feed it fresh river water every week or it would curse us. It was only when I went to an American grocery store for the first time that I realized I'd been praying all my life to a shiitake mushroom."

I was laughing but Vida just shrugged it off and went on with her story. Said that when she and Fito landed at Miami International he disappeared, and some other guys ushered her into a car, stuck a gun into her stomach, and informed her that Fito had sold her for seven thousand dollars that she had to pay off starting now.

I couldn't sleep that night. The boyfriend returned from work exhausted, rolled around next to me, pulled the blankets off of me, pulled me close, trying to initiate more but I feigned indigestion. I couldn't stand the night or his touch. I'd sworn myself to silence, not wanting to betray Vida's confession. If I told the boyfriend, he would tell Sacha, who I was certain would then reject her, since I'd known many a man who loved to hold a girl's past against her.

The boyfriend grew up in a two-room house on a dusty patch of land with chickens that became dinner. His father left his mom when she was pregnant with him and she never remarried. They had a cat that was constantly pregnant, but the kittens always disappeared within days of their birth. When the boyfriend was seven he caught his mother drowning them in a bucket, something that still caused him nightmares. When he took me to the winter carnival that year, we spotted a cat stranded in the middle of the Palmetto Expressway crouched against the highway divider. The boyfriend stopped the car, nearly causing an accident, and ran into the darkness to rescue it. The cat lived with him now and often left decapitated mice on the kitchen floor. "Because he loves me," said the boyfriend. "He knows I saved his life."

The boyfriend was tall, with enormous thigh muscles and a back that was wide and defined like the smooth ripples of the Sahara. He had stretch marks on his biceps from a few cycles of teenage steroids, and more wrinkles around his blue eyes than you'd think a guy his age should have. No matter how many showers he took he still had the musty smell of a workout, and sometimes I left bite marks on his shoulders and neck just to keep the other women away. I didn't used to be this territorial. The boyfriend thought it was cute: a Latin thing.

When he and Sacha convened and fell into their Hungarian slang, sounds and intonations reminding me that we would never really understand each other, I looked to Vida. She was sitting on the lawn chair with her knees curled into her chest, a cigarette propped to her lips by her long red nails.

"They could be brothers," she said.

It was true. They looked like twins with their creamy complexions, shaved heads, and box-smashed noses.

She asked me how I met the boyfriend and I told her the prepackaged story: I was sweating on the treadmill and he picked me up. Most people laughed when I said that but Vida gave me her still eyes, then offered a half smile as if to appease me.

"How did you meet Sacha?"

"You don't know?"

"No."

"The house. He worked there, too. He was the guard."

We were speaking Spanish, so I know that he couldn't have known what we were saying, but Sacha appeared within seconds, pulled Vida up by the elbow, and dragged her toward the driveway. She seemed defiant as he talked into her face. She crossed her arms and looked away, at the ground, up to the sky, even to me on the other side of the yard. When she came back, I asked her if everything was all right and she rolled her eyes as if bored to death. "Such a big production," she said, "just to tell me he loves me."

I was exaggerating before when I said that I had no female friends in Florida. I had one: Jessamy. A thin-lipped strawberry blonde. The kind of gringa that doesn't know what she is but if you ask will probably say Scottish and Welsh. This is odd to me because my parents know our family lines five generations wide and ten generations back, down to the last conquistador.

Jess and I were new teachers together but she couldn't stand it, so she left after a year, got her real estate license, and now all she talked about were interest rates. Usually we'd meet for coffee because she was only willing to break away from her new fiancé for one-hour blocks at a time.

She'd never ask about the boyfriend because she thought he was a loser and whenever she got on my case about him I avoided her for a month or two. I wanted to tell her about Vida because Jess did a stint as a social worker before teaching and I thought she might have something to say about it, but when I started she got that look like she wished I'd cut it and finally said, sighing, "I don't know why you hang around those people, Sabina."

I was pissed but held back. If I hadn't, the first words out of my mouth would be, "I don't want your life, Jess. I'm not like you."

And her next question would be, "Who exactly are you trying to be?"

I wasn't ready for that either.

Later that night, when the boyfriend and I were eating pasta in front of the television, I told him I'd seen Jessamy earlier.

"I don't know why you hang around her," the boyfriend said as if his food had suddenly become spoiled. "That girl has the fear of life in her eyes."

I defended her. Said she was my friend, but the boyfriend wasn't listening. Flipping channels with his free hand, shoveling linguine into his mouth with the other. Afterward, we smoked cigarettes on the balcony and then went to bed. We weren't one of those couples who fall asleep like intertwined roots. We kept to our separate sides of the mattress, only came together to have sex and to push each other out of bed in the morning.

* * *

Vida had many smiles: careful ones, small ones; the harsh but sexy ones she gave Sacha that looked like more of a decoy. But sometimes a sunrise ripped across her face and she smiled like it was going to save her life. Like at the beach or when she spoke of her family. She smiled even when she told me how she worked in a flower shop in El Centro Andino only to give her money to her father who would then gamble it away, and how her brother Tony worked as a mechanic and a messenger for gangsters, and ate every meal with a gun next to his plate, which is why she had no problem with cleaning Sacha's gun for him. She said she had a little sister named Justina who worked in the kitchen of a diplomat's house and they were training her to serve dinner for dignitaries and maybe one day she'd get to work for one of the overseas ambassadors.

Her mom, she said, was a gentle woman who worked as a companion to an old scientist who was going senile. She had to sleep in the old man's house most nights because he had a habit of wandering into the street and had once been lost for two days before Vida's mom recovered him on the steps of the Gold Museum talking about Bolívar to anyone who would listen.

It was Vida's mother who encouraged her to be a beauty queen and made Vida's competition dresses herself. And Vida had paid off, winning Reina de la Primavera, Reina de

Azúcar, Reina de las Flores, and even Reina de Usme. People said she had a gift; even her priest said she had been blessed with beauty to bring money to her family. Back then, she said, all she hoped for was a regional title. But then Fito put it in her head that she needed to aim higher: Miami. "The Jerusalem for Colombians" is how she put it. Enter shiitake mushroom.

We were at the beach by Forty-first Street. I was on a school break and the boyfriend was at work. I still didn't know what Sacha's day job was and gave up asking. Vida and I were stretched across towels in our bikinis and she stared into the sky as if she could see her whole history projected into the clouds like a movie screen.

Two or three times, guys wandered over to our spot of sand and tried to flirt, but Vida cursed them, inspiring some insults about how we were stuck-up sluts, but she just laughed.

"I hate men most of the time," she told me.

I asked her how she ended up with Sacha, said that they seemed like a good couple, which was only a half-lie.

"There were four of us and we each had a bedroom. Sacha sat in the waiting area most of the time. Collected money. Watched for police. Made sure that we didn't try to escape. But I could see that he liked me. I worked at earning his trust. It was obvious that he was lonely. It wasn't so hard, Sabina. You can get a lonely person to do anything."

She paused, lit herself a fresh cigarette.

"It took a year but one day he said he loved me and that he wanted us to be together like normal people, away from the house. He gave the other girls money so they could run away and the two of us left together. We had to hide for months because his boss had people searching everywhere. But time passed. And now we are okay."

My friend Jess would say it was the freak factor that drew me to Vida. That she was a novelty act for me, a living movie complete with exploitation of Latinas. There was also the vanity element, that, in her, I saw a parallel life, one that my mother always imagined aloud: the What if we had stayed to live in Colombia? narrative. She always said I would have grown up more feminine, with better manners, and that probably I would have figured out how to be married by now.

And then there were the Colombian horror stories that my parents and their expatriate friends told one another whenever they got together for sancocho and vallenatos, to appease their guilt for having left the motherland.

"Un país de locos!" The men would shake their heads in shame, repeating headlines ripped from *El Tiempo* about the guerrilla and paramilitary infiltrating the cities. Political corruption, secuestros, executions, baby trafficking, child prostitutes. The land-mine capital of the world.

"Que verguenza," Papi would say as if talking about an alcoholic parent.

My parents and their friends all congratulated themselves for having American-raised kids who only had to see Colombia on vacation. The last time I'd been back was at nineteen, spending two weeks at tea parties with the old relatives, who liked to speak French to one another for kicks, and the cousins, who hung out at El Country and made it their mission to get me wasted on aguardiente in La Zona Rosa every night of the week.

Then there was my tía's muchacha, Claribel, who had a secret history we weren't supposed to mention that involved getting raped by a half brother at fourteen, resulting in a baby who was adopted by an Italian family. Claribel, who had to put in a good two years of service before my aunt would pay for her to get her high school diploma on Saturday mornings. Claribel, who drifted through the rooms of my aunt's house like a ghost, making our beds and shining our shoes without our asking.

"Do you ever think of going back?" I finally asked Vida.

"Every day. But first I have to think of a story to tell my family, to explain what I've been doing here all this time."

* * *

Dolor ajena is what they call it. Feeling pain on behalf of someone else. A pain that is not your own. No succinct way to say it in English. I suppose that's how we get by.

I'm not that charitable. Nothing in me said I should help Vida. Give her money from my savings so she could buy a plane ticket back home. Hook her up with a counselor at my school, someone to talk her through her dramas. Help her heal. None of that. I just wanted to drink her up like everyone else.

She asked me if I had some old clothes that I could give her. Hers were worn-through, so that the seams on her jeans looked as if they might give at any moment. I never wore clothes enough for them to disintegrate from wear. Always tossed them on a whim to make room for more. I showed up at her place with three shopping bags' worth and she pored through my clothes like they were spun from gold, trying things on and modeling them in her dumpy living room. Sacha was in the bedroom, supposedly on the phone with a client. They had a small balcony that opened onto a back parking lot and the kitchenette smelled like grease.

She walked across the room like it was a runway, posed, and for a second I got a glimpse of that beauty queen. Her prize smile, lashes that fluttered their way into a judge's favorable graces.

She was wearing a blue dress with an arabesque print. A dress I bought in a Las Olas boutique and never wore. It hung in my closet for a year waiting for a party, a romantic summer dinner, nights that never happened. It looked like it was made for Vida; the gauzy fabric clung to her round breasts and draped off her behind like the bows of a palm tree.

The only way she could think to thank me was by doing my nails for me. She pulled out a plastic tub, filled it with water and soap and washed my feet for me in a way that made me ashamed. She was proud of herself, telling me she already knew how to do all the stuff that they teach at the beauty academy. She'd cruise right through it, she said, be their best student ever, just as soon as Sacha gave her the money to enroll.

She chose the color polish. A light pink because she said I struck her as an understated sort of girl.

"A natural shade," she said, "because it's quiet and honest. Like you."

And this only made me feel like more of a phony.

The boyfriend slept with another girl. I asked him straight out and he confessed. Said it happened twice and that it was another lady from the gym. Forty. Divorced twice. Panamanian. I know because I asked for details and I was so angry my only response was, "Panama used to be Colombia, asshole."

Then, my canned defense. Said I hoped it was worth it. You lost me. Lost me. Lost me. Gave him a wall of silence, unreturned phone calls, adjusted to my life without him, the hole in my evenings, and the cold bed. Returned to life before the Hungarian. Sunday without his grill. His friends. Without Vida, the living documentary.

And then I caved in, because I am like everyone else who can't do anything based on real principles. I thought of my father. How he would shake his head and say I have no character. That he didn't raise me for this kind of treatment from a man. And when my parents called to check up on me, I closed my eyes and mumbled that everything was fine, while the boyfriend fell asleep with his head in my lap like nothing.

When I saw Vida again, this time for dinner, the four of us at a churrascaria on Seventy-ninth, she and I fell into our Spanish while the boys talked business in their language.

"I didn't think you would take him back," she said softly.

"Neither did I."

Later, the boys suggested we get a bottle of wine and drink it on the beach. Normally, Vida loved the beach, but with Sacha and the boyfriend there she seemed indifferent. As the boys got drunk and did flips in the sand, Vida lit herself cigarette after cigarette. She had an eye on Sacha while he and the boyfriend frolicked like little boys. He blew her a kiss and she stared back under a veil that looked a lot like contempt.

"The owners of the house used to surprise us at night sometimes. Once, they went extra hard on me, punched my eyes so that I couldn't open them for days. I never was allowed out except two or three times when Sacha let me smoke a cigarette with him behind the house. But after that beating, he put me on his motorcycle and all I felt was the wind because I couldn't see. I held him as tight as I could but I was in so much pain I thought for sure I would fall off and die on the road. And then I smelled the change in the air. Salty and sweet at once and he carried me into the water. At first it stung but then I opened my eyes and saw the sea in front of me, all around me. We were in our clothes but wet up to our necks. He held me so I could float, didn't talk so I could listen to only the waves. And when he returned me to the house and put me back into the bedroom where I lived, I thought, It's not his fault that he is so cruel. We'd all become different creatures."

Just as I started to think of her and Sacha as some kind of weird fairy tale, Vida turned to me and declared that she was no Eréndira.

She told me other things.

She said there were four girls and they were expected to see clients whenever they showed up, and could only sleep a few hours at a time. One of the girls wore bikinis all the time and would do anything for drugs, and the owner of the house, a guy named Raul, kept her supplied. One girl, Vida told me, hardly ever spoke and once they raped her so badly that she bled for hours in the shower. There was a woman doctor who came to see the girls when Sacha called, but she was pitiless and Vida was pretty sure all the girls were sterilized during one of those brutal examinations. Vida heard of a girl who was there before her, who managed to have a client fall in love with her and buy her debt to the house. Some girls thought she was like a Cinderella but Vida thought the client probably made the girl his personal slave. Vida said the other girls resented that Sacha took a liking to her, that she tried to explain to them that she had a plan for seducing him to get them all free, but that Sacha started encouraging clients to pick other girls so Vida wouldn't have to work. For this, Vida said, she would never forgive herself.

One of the clients let Vida use his cell phone to call her parents, but when she heard her father's voice she hung up. She said she lived in her dreams for a long time. Thought of her old boyfriend, Fernando, who moved to Brooklyn to be with his father when they were still in high school. He'd written her a few times but the letters stopped and Vida told herself that when she was finally free, she'd go find him. "And then the beatings," she said. "Every time the bruises faded, there came another round."

It never occurred to me to ask Vida where this house of horrors was. I never thought to report it to the police, see if the house was still in operation. Help her expose Fito, maybe help the girls who would follow.

None of that. I just listened.

That New Year's Eve, the Hungarians had a party in a mansion on Hibiscus Island. The owners were off skiing and one of the boyfriend's friends was the caretaker, lived in the guesthouse, and had run of the place when the patrons were away. We drank champagne on the boat dock, watched the fireworks over Biscayne Bay. The boyfriend pulled me to his side as we sat on the concrete ledge, our toes skimming the dark canal water. We had our midnight kiss, hugged all the friends. Vida wrapped her skinny arms around my neck and we toasted privately to the future.

On our way home, I asked the boyfriend if he knew that Vida used to be a prostitute and that Sacha was her warden.

He didn't lift his eyes from the causeway. Just nodded, palms closing tighter around the steering wheel.

"I don't know how she can stand to be with him."

The boyfriend looked over at me, a shot of anger in his eyes. "He almost got killed because of her. They hunted him for months."

"He watched them beat her, rape her, and sell her."

"She never tried to escape."

"They shot a girl in the back once for trying to run away."

He laughed. "They just told the girls that to keep them from trying."

"How could you have known about it all and done nothing?"

That set him off. The boyfriend pulled over right there on the Venetian Causeway and wrapped his fat knuckles around my shoulder, his rough fingertips carving into my skin.

"It was just a job, Sabina. He had to make a living, too. It's not his fault they took her there. If it wasn't for him she'd still be there."

"Being a witness can make a person just as guilty."

A solid minute passed. The boyfriend's eyes drove into mine and I refused to soften. He wasn't my lover anymore but an accomplice to something terrible and his hands felt like weights on my body. The strange thing is that he was looking at me with a blend of hatred and confusion. We didn't recognize each other anymore. Or maybe we were seeing each other for the first time.

"Get out of the car, Sabina."

As soon as he said it, he relented. Pulled me into his chest with that same heavy hand and pushed my hair off my face, kissing my cheeks and forehead with his dry, chapped lips.

I wish I'd gotten out, had a little honor and walked home by foot, each step reminding me how off-track I was in my life. But I didn't move. Let the boyfriend drive me home and let him sleep in my bed and everything else.

Vida and I both woke up the next day with the same idea. She called me while the boyfriend was still sleeping and Sacha was out for an errand for one of his clients.

She didn't even have to say it. I already knew.

Later that afternoon she told Sacha she was going to buy cigarettes. I told the boyfriend I was visiting Jessamy. I picked Vida up on the corner of her block and we drove all the way to Orlando before we stopped for a toilet. Didn't talk the whole way, either. It was only then that we realized we needed a plan.

We drove for something like thirty hours. When we got to the New Jersey line I called my parents and said to expect us. They were nice to my new friend Vida, and didn't ask why they'd never heard of her, or what we were doing there in New Jersey in the dead of January with no luggage and still in our Miami clothes. I dressed her up in one of my high school sweaters, gave her some thick socks and duck boots. Made her look like a real suburbanite.

I slept in my childhood bedroom and she slept next door in the one that belonged to my brother. I went into my parents' room early the next morning and shut the door behind me. Vida was still sleeping. I tried to explain to them as much as I could but stopped short in several places, every time I saw my mother lift her palm to cover her heart.

I'm a coward. I hid when my parents took Vida into the kitchen, pushed some breakfast her way, and tried to talk some truth out of her while the maid, Luz, pretended to be busy chopping vegetables for the lunch soup.

I listened from the hallway as Vida complimented the coffee and asked for another bagel. My mother told her she could use our phone to call her parents and Vida declined.

"They must be worried about you," said Papi.

I knew that's all it would take. The face of a father. Any father.

Vida started to cry and Papi had an in. Offered her a ticket home. Or, he said, she could stay here and they'd figure something else out. But my mother pushed her toward Colombia. Said it's not a question of dreams anymore. It's a question of love and she should be with her family.

Seems so easy now. After all those confessions on the beach. Problems solved by a long drive and my dad's credit card.

The next day, she was home.

On my end, I still hadn't figured anything out, but I decided to stay with my parents a little while longer. The boyfriend would forget me after a while. Maybe he'd pester me to find out about Vida for Sacha, but he'd replace me with another chica soon enough.

My parents and I took her to Newark Airport together for that insanely early Avianca flight. I insisted to Papi that he book her a direct flight, no layover in Miami. I was afraid the sight of the ocean might blow her off course. It happens to the best of us.

She hugged me. Gave me a new smile. A shy one I'd never seen before. Thanked me for nothing specific, which was fine because I felt like I'd been really stingy in every way. Why did it take me this long to get her here? I'll never know.

When she landed, she called. Her parents got on the phone and thanked mine for their help. They still didn't have a clue about Vida's life here. I wondered if she'd ever tell them.

It's been a year since all this.

I went back to Miami. After a few failed phone calls the boyfriend forgot me, just as predicted. I only saw him once afterward, at the movies. I was alone and he was with a girl wearing knee-high leather boots in the middle of Florida summer.

Every time I get to thinking of Vida, she is the one to call first. Always that fuzzy connection, her warning me that she's only got a few minutes left on the calling card and we might get cut off.

"I'm just calling to make sure you're okay," she tells me. "I worry about you."

That always cracks me up.

She says she's washing hair at a nice salon on La Septima, and they're going to teach her how to do highlights. Her family is planning a trip to Cartagena. Their first vacation together ever.

She sends her love to my parents. Makes me promise to visit her one of these days.

On the long drive up from Miami, Vida and I went through two or three states without a word between us. She hardly moved her gaze from the stretch of interstate sound barriers beyond her window. Somewhere around Maryland, Vida spoke over the hum of the engine that comforted me through the night: "There is no love. Only people living life together. Tomorrow will be better."

DÍA

I find him sitting on a plastic lounge chair by the hotel pool. I give a little wave and he stands. We kiss on the cheek. He tells me I'm taller than he remembers.

"Sit down, sit down," he offers just as thunder rolls in, so we find a spot on an iron bench under a flaking white gazebo.

"It's been a long time," he says.

We were never a couple. Still, it felt that way because Día was always mad at me. I tell him that, thinking it'll go over like a joke, but he just stares at me like he doesn't remember it like that. He called a few days ago, the first time in five years, to say he was coming to Miami and he heard from Malik and some others that I live here now.

"I tried to say good-bye," I say. "You never picked up the phone."

"You were always good about those sorts of things."

Día looks like life ran him over. Must have dropped twenty pounds, melting into his blue button-down, and his black pants have all kinds of shadow spots on them. The Día

I remember had soccer legs and sharp shoulders, but now he looks gelatinous, eyes twitching, mestizo skin yellowed, hair knotted in buds. While he talks about the humidity, how he can't understand how a civilized person can live here, I look for the rod he used to have in his tongue, a tiny barbell that got in the way every time we kissed.

I don't see it.

I ask what brings him to town and he's agitated, looking to the dark clouds for the right words.

"You're not going to like it," he says.

"Just tell me."

I think it can't be that bad because Día was never one for drugs. He managed a bar for years without drinking, spending the slow afternoons before the happy-hour crew rolled in reading history books on a stool in the corner. That's how we met. One day I asked what he was reading.

"I'm a professional gambler," he says.

I can't help it, my whole forehead lifts like strings are tugging.

Last time I saw Día, he was studying for the Foreign Service exam. Spoke six languages and could talk politics and literature in any of them, always on my back to study, asking what grades I was pulling since I was majoring in screwing around. He'd yell at me on the corner of Fourteenth, tell me a smart girl like me was throwing it all away. Call me an ingrate, a brat, a blind fool for running around with Malik, who Día said spent more time in the bathroom snorting the amputated limbs of my compatriots than being a boyfriend to me.

"Gambling?"

Día explains that he started playing blackjack online and then joined some secret league in the city. His eyes shine when he tells me he realized he has a gift, cashing out every night with thousands, way more than the small wads he earned at the bar.

It's been too long for me to play the friend, tease him, ask him what happened to Mr. Integrity. I'm just looking at his pallid face, bushy brows wiggling while he tries to explain poker like it's a peace treaty, full of rehearsed rationale.

He came down to Florida to play the Indian casinos. Was at the one in Seminole till five this morning. He moved out of the Astoria place and has a loft on the Bowery now, though he hardly ever leaves except to play poker in Bay Ridge. He's got standing matches online a few nights a week against people all over the world; the Koreans are tough to beat, he says, and some guy in Australia is the reigning king. But Día grows taller for a second, tells me he's ranked fourth in the world.

"It's a really big deal, gatîna," he tells me and when I hear his old name for me I notice his voice has changed—used to be deep and lush, like the voice of that guy who sings on Tuesdays at the Carioca place on First. Now it's hollow, scratchy, creaking as if he's not used to speaking so much anymore, and even though we're looking out at the beach, it feels like we're in an empty apartment.

When he's through he says, "So what do you think?"

I know my smile is so weak not even Día buys it. He offers me a cigarette but I tell him I quit years ago.

We used to smoke together. Sitting on the radiator of my place on Fourteenth, blowing smoke out the window, watching each other. We were just friends at the time, had dropped the kissing part because I was with Malik now. "I don't understand what you guys talk about" was Día's favorite line, and just to piss him off I'd say that was the best part— Malik and I didn't talk about anything.

I used to wear these big hoop earrings, my hair down to my hips, supertight jeans, and blouses with embroidery like I was some kind of gitana—a full dimension away from the teacher garb I'm wearing now. I used to take photos, mostly of city people with sad faces, and sometimes Malik would tear off his shirt, lay against a brick wall showing off his wingspan, flexing his back to carve a new landscape for my camera. Malik, with his Egyptian curls and lion tattoo stretching across his shoulder blades, a guy who couldn't plan past next week. It was Día's idea to curate my first show right there in the bar. Threw me a party and everything, but when I tried to introduce him to my friends, Día hung back and stayed in his corner.

Día asks me if I ever think about moving back, and before the question is all the way out, I'm shaking my head.

"I wonder if I could stand to live here," he says, sticking his palm out into the curtain of rain.

I look at my watch.

"Somewhere you need to be?"

I feel bad. Say no, I've got time. Let's finish this thing.

We play catch up, start each sentence with "Remember when."

Día asks me if Malik and I still talk and I say no.

"Why did you split up anyway?"

"You know."

He wants to hear me say it even if he heard the story long ago from the people on the block. How Malik hit me in plain sight because I was on his case about the coke. Punched me in the face so hard I landed on a little girl blowing up balloons on her Third Avenue stoop. The little girl cried and by the time I got to my feet, missing two teeth, Malik was around the corner. Some Honduran deli guys saw the whole thing, cleaned me up, wiped my face, told me they'd take me to the station to press charges but I said no. Told the dentist I fell. I went into hiding. Thought maybe Día would come looking for me but he never did. I hated him for that. But I never told him.

Día tells me that after I left, he went back to Brazil. Got sick of New York and had this feeling he needed to be among his people. Taught English at a bunch of different schools, rented a great apartment in São Paulo for cheap, had a car and everything. But New York called to him. He returned to the same apartment in Astoria, the same job pouring drinks for the same drunk idiots. Got married in between, then divorced, just a few months ago, from that girl he hired as a cocktail waitress around the time I started up with Malik. Asks me if I remember her. I don't.

"She remembers you," he says.

I recognize those eyes from back when he used to grab my arm in the bar, tell me to stop drinking, to go home like a normal girl and stop spending my nights with degenerates. "You're so judgmental," I used to tell him and Día looked like he might fold over and cry.

It's raining all around us. Heavy sheets more like walls as we sit on the bench under the gazebo. There's nowhere to go. Not without getting drenched down to our skin.

Día tells me the wife forbid him from reaching out to me all these years. She sensed his thing with me ran deeper than cigarettes and nerdy conversations in the corner of the bar. I don't know what to say. He's looking at me like this is what he came here for and I wish the rain would stop already.

"Tell me about your life."

"You know," I say. "Nothing special."

"Boyfriend?"

"Not anymore."

"You always had a few in rotation."

There was a time when I wanted it to be Día. Only Día. When I wanted him to wipe that crabby look off his face and tell me something real, not one of his theories about the world. He used to mock me. Make me list all the things I believe in. God, Heaven, the inherent goodness of mankind—and then he'd laugh, give me reasons why none of these things exist. We'd sit together in the park, our thighs smacking against each other on the bench while breakdancers and skateboarders rocked their bodies nearby. He'd talk about the world, everything that was wrong with it. Sometimes I listened. Sometimes I wished he'd just mellow out and take me home, lie on the bed next to me, and be still and quiet so we could fall asleep together. I waited. But it never happened. We never spent a single night that way.

Then I met Malik, who pulled me by the wrist into the phone booth one night and told me to be his girl. Día was watching from behind the bar when I let Malik kiss me.

"Why did you come?" Día asks me.

"To see an old friend. Catch up."

"Is that all?"

"Día."

We let that sit. The rain relents and sun cleaves the sky. I can't stand it anymore. I get up, tell him I'm going. He doesn't move. Just like me to run away. Just like him not to do much to stop me. When I'm on the other side of the pool, I look back at Día sitting there lighting another cigarette. I wonder why we never fit. Why we never tried.

MADRE PATRIA

My mother was telling my father she had that dream again—the one about the dying horse. It wasn't a dream so much as a memory that came to her in sleep: She was nine years old, riding in the passenger's seat of her father's Chevrolet as he drove her and her sisters to the farm in Fusagasugá. On one of the long, dusty roads of the savanna Mami saw a gray horse walking along the ridge of grass—so thin you could count every rib, his back sunken as if he were carrying a thousand ghosts. The horse wobbled along, unsure of every step, and Mami begged her father to stop the car, said the poor horse was starving and that they needed to feed it, give it some of the fruit they had packed in a basket in the back of the car, give it some of the water they had brought in bottles all the way from the capital. But Mami's father said, Don't worry, my darling, the horse is fine, just bored and tired. Told her they had to get to la finca before dark or some guerrilleros might stop them on the road and start some trouble.

Mami cried, told her father the horse would die and it would be their fault, but her father kept driving, promising her that they'd come back this way tomorrow on their way to pick up some new chickens for the farm. He'd drive the trailer and said if the horse was still there, they'd bring him back with them and have one of the ranch hands nurse him to health. My mother didn't sleep all night, waiting for her father to have his morning tinto and his first cigarette before he was ready to get back on the road to find the horse. When they came to the same spot, the horse was still there, lying dead on the grass, its mouth wide open with flies gathered at its nostrils.

Mami told Papi the dream like it was the first time, and he listened, detail by detail. Finally, he told her that it was because we were in Colombia that she was falling into nightmares. Papi hated coming to Colombia, always said this place never did him any favors, and it was only because Mami's sister was here that we ever came back.

"This country is a giant cemetery," Papi said. In a way it was true, most everyone Mami had ever loved here was dead. Every visit to Bogotá was marked by a full day of leaving flowers at the tombstones of relatives I never met, including Mami's parents.

Mami got mad when he talked like that, said they were both born of Andean earth and we should honor it.

"Es que no entiendes, Maria. This country doesn't want us back."

On the cot next to me, my brother pretended to sleep. We were assigned to our cousin Símon's room. He and my prima Sara preferred to bunk with each other in Sara's room rather than be with either one of us. Even though we were all close in age, us kids didn't know what to say to one another most of the time. Símon and Sara were four and six, and Carmen was going through this phase of dressing her kids in lederhosen and embroidered jumpers as if they lived in the Swiss Alps or something.

I poked Cris with my finger. "Do you hear them?" I knew he was awake. He always kept his eyes closed for a long time after he was conscious in the morning just to eavesdrop on the world. I was seven and Cris was ten but he had skipped a year of school and this always made him seem much older to me.

"I'm not deaf," he answered, eyes still shut.

My aunt's house was cold. The climate is static in Bogotá: always cool with only a taunting sun breaking through the fog of the Andes. But they didn't have heaters and Tía Carmen insisted that it wasn't because she was cheap—nobody in Bogotá had them. So we slept under alpaca blankets so heavy that we couldn't move all night, packed into the mattress as if we were being smuggled.

Mami and Papi were silent on the other side of the wall. Carmen gave them the guest room, which was furnished with things that used to be in Mami's childhood home. Every time we visited she would say, "So that's where that dresser ended up," or "I remember that lamp." It annoyed Carmen, who said it made her feel like Mami was accusing her of theft, and they always got into a big fight that resulted in both of them crying and the husbands trying to calm them down.

Carmen would tell Mami that she had changed and that the United States had turned her into another kind of woman. This made Mami cry even more and it always took her ages to fall asleep, with Papi offering her words so soft I couldn't make them out through that flimsy wall. Cris always fell asleep the minute he hit the mattress but I stayed awake for hours listening to the sounds of the apartment, the car horns on the carretera below, the echoes of a city I didn't know.

On nights that our parents went out for dinner with old friends or distant cousins, the primos, Cris and I were left with a family who lived in the same building. The older couple had a daughter named Carla, who kept us entertained until our parents came to collect us. Carla was eighteen, beautiful, with golden skin and canela hair. She had tiny green eyes, a flattened nose, and a pale coin-size smile that looked so fragile it might fall off her face. She was slight of build and always wore a denim jacket that her mother said made her look like a campesina. If you put her in a lineup, compared her to other girls the way people like to do, you might not think her so pretty, but I thought Carla was the most spectacular girl I'd ever seen in real life, with the largest laugh you could imagine coming from such a small face.

She went to school at Los Andes, was studying psychology, and wanted to help children. Maybe that's why she would ask me so many questions. Not the usual stream that I got in Colombia about what it was like to live in Gringolandia. Carla wanted to know what I was afraid of and what my dreams were. I told her I only had one dream that I remembered and that was of my brother killing my only friend, Mina, who lived down the block. In my dream, my brother locked Mina inside a refrigerator until she suffocated. The dream was so real that I avoided Cris for days afterward every time I had it. And my only fear, I told Carla, was of losing my parents the way Mami had lost hers, before they had a chance to see her make anything of her life.

"How are you afraid of them dying? By sickness? By murder?"

Cris and the primos were watching a movie on television while Carla and I sat on the window seat overlooking the street.

"I'm afraid that one day they'll just disappear."

Carla nodded as if she understood what I meant. She told me to wait for her a minute, walked off toward her bedroom, and returned with a guitar. She sat beside me again and began strumming. This pulled Cris and the primos away from the movie, and they gathered around Carla, who was already deep into a ranchera.

Cris asked her to play "Purple Rain" but Carla said she didn't know the song by heart. The primos requested some song, and finally I thought of one other than "Los Pollitos Dicen," which was the only Spanish song I really knew.

"'Spanish Eyes,'" I offered and Carla asked me why I wanted that song.

"That's the song that was playing when Mami and Papi had their first dance," I said. "When he was still engaged to that other lady."

Carla's eyes narrowed on me and she asked me what I knew about that.

"She used to sew handkerchiefs for Papi with her own hair, but Papi never wanted to marry her in the first place."

My primos and Cris wanted me to shut up so Carla would play the song already but she kept staring at me as if I was some kind of exhibit. Finally, she pulled her eyes off me and went back to her guitar, sang "Spanish Eyes" in her private-school English, and we all chimed in at the *si, si* part and cried out like mariachis.

She retired the guitar after that song and we all moved to the sofa to watch the rest of the movie, but I fell asleep, and when I woke up, I was buried under the alpaca blanket in Carmen's house with the whispers of my parents on the other side of the wall.

In New Jersey, my brother and I disappeared from our house for hours without having to check in with our parents. We lived on a shaded suburban block near some woods and a river, and played on the slow street with the neighborhood kids until we each got called home to dinner. We rode our bicycles, played Manhunt, sold lemonade, and performed magic shows for each other. My brother was obsessed with *Electric Boogaloo* and spent his afternoons popping, locking, and trying to do backspins and flares on a flattened cardboard box in the driveway with his friends, while I roller-skated up and down the sidewalk convinced I was training for the Olympics. But in Bogotá, we couldn't leave the apartment without an adult escort, and when they took us out it was with their large hands pulling us along the avenida. Carmen took us to the mall one day and along the road there were children, not much older than me, with glazed eyeballs like zombies, asking for money. Every now and then one would poke their nose inside their jacket and lift their head with an even smokier expression than before. I don't know where he heard it but Cris said those kids were sniffing glue, not like the kind we use in art class at school but one that makes you dream and forget where you are.

"Where are their parents?" I asked my brother.

"They don't have any, stupid."

Everywhere, we saw children. On the steps of the cathedral, outside El Andino, perched like gargoyles on the walls of La Zona Rosa. Some of them were selling gum or flowers, and some just floated along the street watching us, saying "Por favor," in low voices. Mami kept telling Carmen the city had changed so much, but Carmen said, "No, mija, it was always like this."

The mothers took us kids for fast food because Cris and I were sick of the ajíaco at home. Mami saved our leftovers to give to a pack of stray dogs we saw circling the parking lot. But behind the dogs came a cluster of children, asking Mami if she had any more scraps for them. We sat in the car with Carmen while Mami went back in to buy the kids some food. Cris, the primos, and I were silent while the kids—you couldn't tell the boys from the girls—stood around the car looking at us, dirt on their faces, mocos like webs around their nostrils, mumbling words I couldn't understand.

*   *   *

Carmen's husband, my Tío Emilio, organized outings for us while my parents and Carmen did their social rounds. He took us to the top of Monserrate, where Cris and I threw up in the cable car, and to the Gold Museum, and when Cris complained that he wanted to go bowling, Emilio took us to a decrepit alley in las afueras. One day, he decided to take us kids to the salt mines while my parents and Carmen went to visit an uncle who Mami had avoided for the last ten years. We roamed around the caves, whispered into the walls that my uncle said could carry voices for miles, and in the old days that was how people would communicate to each other that they were being invaded. Emilio broke off a piece of wall and licked it, helped each of us do the same so we could taste the salty rock, chew it, and when we were through my uncle grinned, "There, niños, you just ate a piece of our land." We giggled because it felt like we were breaking some kind of law.

I liked my uncle a lot. He was tall, gangly, with thick, black glasses and a giant mouth that made me think of alligators. His thick graying hair was slicked back and he was always talking about jazz music and books because his father was a famous writer that the whole country worshipped. The big secret was that Emilio had been working on his own book for years already, late at night after everyone was asleep. Since I often stayed awake, I'd hear him clanking away on the typewriter in his office and smelled his cigarettes because he always smoked as he wrote.

Emilio had his own daughter, but when I was around he was extra special with me. He held my hand and pulled me around the salt mine and said, "All this is part of your inheritance."

"We own this?" I asked, confused.

"All this land belongs to all of us. The good and the bad."

I didn't know what he meant but that night I got a better idea of it. Over dinner, the adults were talking about La Violencia and La Situación. It was the mideighties and the name Escobar was just starting to catch the current. Emilio, a lawyer by trade, told Papi that the man who had already taken over Medellín and was now infiltrating the rest of the country had his hand in every pot and a bounty on the heads of the police and important officials. Papi laughed, said that he couldn't believe it, that he knew Pablito Escobar from childhood. They'd gone to the same school but Papi was a few years older. Still, even then, Papi said, the kid had gangster tendencies.

"His hands are all over this country," Emilio said. "You watch. There's not one pure soul left."

* * *

One of Mami's cousins came to see us at Carmen's house and kept saying how dark Cris and I were. We looked at each other, and even Cris, who always had a retort, didn't know what to say. Another friend, an older lady with orange hair, said I was fat and Cris had bad teeth. Another couple, who insisted on speaking in phony British accents, asked my mother why she allowed us to dress like vagrants. For the next day of visitors Mami had us dress as if we were going to a party and Cris and I sat around the living room stiffly, him in his First Communion suit and me in a fluffy dress, sighing that we wanted to go back to New Jersey.

Since we were groomed better, the criticisms turned to Mami. One of her relatives asked her what country club she belonged to and Mami said ninguno. The man raised his furry brows as if he'd just witnessed a scandal. He asked Mami what charities she belonged to and Mami said ninguno, that she was taking college classes and helping out at Papi's factory. The man just about lost it. Told her he couldn't imagine why she left Colombia to live como una cualquiera in New Jersey.

He was sweating, and asked Carmen's maid for a glass of water.

Mami softened her face. I could tell she was trying to show this guy respect, though for the life of me, I couldn't figure out how we were related to him.

"It's different over there," Mami said. "We manage just fine. And we are happy."

"How can you be happy," the man challenged, "when you're invisible?"

Luckily Papi was out with Emilio or he would have let the guy have it. Papi already knew that Mami's Bogotá society gang thought he was a renegade Paisa; he didn't finish high school and even though he had a profitable business in the States, he was a factory man, not one of those guys from El Club who get siphoned off to the American Ivy Leagues and then return to be senators. Plus Papi's accent gave him away, fluttery and still carrying the heat of Medellín, not with a potato in the mouth like the Cachaco accent. And even though all those people talked about Papi like he was a bumpkin and not a big-time empresario, they never hesitated to ask him for a loan—showing up at Carmen's house saying, "Amigo, I've got a proposition for you. All I need is a little capital."

"Where were they," Papi would ask Mami, "when we had cardboard boxes for furniture?"

That night, Papi came home a little drunk with Emilio. Mami was already in bed when he went into the room and I heard him drop his watch on the night table.

The whispers started. Then Mami's voice grew louder, clearer. I looked to my brother who was already sleeping, his mouth open and lips dry.

"I was *somebody* here," Mami whimpered.

"What are you saying?" Papi was impatient, like he just wanted to sleep.

"Quiero volver."

Mami had always wanted to move back. Her saying so was nothing new. I wanted to wake up Cris, tell him what I'd heard, ask him if it was really true that we were nobodies in New Jersey. Ask him why Mami seemed so disappointed by her American life, if it was because my brother and I spoke funny Spanish and were always messing up our tenses, or maybe because in New Jersey, store people were always saying to Mami, "I can't understand you, ma'am. Speak English," and my mother would shoot back slow and steady, "I *am* speaking English." I wanted to ask him why Mami spoke as if Papi stole her from Colombia, as if she belonged more to this country than to us.

But then my parents went quiet and I decided it was best to try and sleep.

Carla invited my cousins, Cris, and me to her apartment to make arepas. It was the day before Easter and our parents took the opportunity to go visit some other ancient relatives because Papi said they would probably croak before our next trip back. One was the million-year-old third wife of Mami's great-uncle, whom he married when she was only fifteen. Mami said the woman was pretty much senile now but that didn't take away from their gesture of driving all the way out to Chicó to bring her cakes and cheeses.

Símon, who at four was the youngest of us, refused to make arepas because in his own house men were not allowed in the kitchen, so Carla planted him in front of the TV again. Sara, who thought herself Símon's bodyguard, went with him and Cris decided he didn't want to cook either so he chose the television as well. This left Carla and me in the quiet of her kitchen. The muchachas were watching telenovelas in their rooms and her parents were out.

I told Carla about the discussion I overheard between my parents the night before and she nodded as she listened.

"Women cut off their hands for men," Carla said as we patted our balls of flour into flat disks and dropped them onto the pan. I was already quite good at making arepas and Carla even said so. I told her I had learned from Papi's mother, Abuela Luna with the violet eyes, who lived a few miles from us in New Jersey.

"What do you mean they cut off their hands?"

She shook her head as if she wished she could take back her words. I still didn't understand what she meant and she didn't explain. We went on in silence, sculpting our arepas, trying to make each one more perfectly round, flat, and smooth than the one before.

Carla had a boyfriend nobody knew about. Nobody except me. She confessed her secret to me the day of the arepas when my brother and cousins had all fallen into a deep sleep in the living room. Carla and I were on the window seat again. She asked me if I had a boyfriend and I said no, I was only seven, and then when I asked her, she blushed, said his name was Andy and he was a professor at her university.

"Is he old?"

"No, he's just thirty," she said, which sounded very old to me.

"He rides a motorcycle," she went on, her eyes widening so that it looked like her emeralds would roll right out from under her lashes. "He was engaged when I met him and he left that girl for me. My parents don't know yet but we're going to get married."

Her little mouth grew bigger and bigger. Her teeth glistened, her cheeks filled with color, and her smile expanded so much I could nearly see down her throat.

"How do you know he loves you?" I asked her.

"It's a feeling," she said. "No matter where I am, with him I feel that I'm home."

I wanted to tell her I felt the same way about our cocker spaniel, Manchas, but I was shy. Carla told me her Andy said he'd been waiting his whole life for her and I wondered how that could be since he didn't even know she existed until last semester. Even so, I felt privileged that she told me her secret, especially as us kids filed back down to Carmen's apartment after the parents came to get us. They still wore sleep on their faces but I was refreshed because I felt I'd been let in on the adult world of love, and the way people talk about it, like it's some kind of secret code.

On Easter morning, Mami and Carmen were each in their rooms crying as the husbands tended to them. They got in a huge fight about something that happened when they were kids. It all came out over breakfast, when Carmen asked Mami why she wears so much makeup and Mami snapped that it might be because her sisters told her she was ugly her whole life.

It continued from there and us kids went into the living room to play with the pollitos Emilio bought off some guy on the street. There was a basket full of chicks sitting on a mound of fake grass, each one dyed a different color: pink, blue, green, or orange. A whole rainbow of pollitos that chirped as they bounced around between us and crapped in our laps. We each took one and named it. Cris named his blue one Rambo and Sara named hers Flor. Símon named his Símon and Cris told him it was stupid to name a pollito after yourself but Símon said the chick was actually named after Bolívar so it was perfectly acceptable. I named my orange pollito New Jersey.

While we went to Easter mass, we left the pollitos in the bathroom. I thought they would get cold, so I dragged the alpaca blanket off my bed and tried to leave it there for them, but Carmen stopped me, said the blanket was very expensive and did not belong on the bathroom floor. After mass, the pollitos were gone. Emilio explained that someone took them to live on a finca. Not the one in Fusagasugá that belonged to Mami's father—she lost it to some relative in a family inheritance land war years earlier, which turned out to be a blessing because guerrilleros had taken to hanging around on that land and when they get rowdy, they sometimes cut off people's fingers, ears, or tongues. I heard that last part on the television in Carmen's house.

My cousins and I were crying over the lost pollitos. Even Cris was sad over losing Rambo so soon. We'd fallen in love with those little chicks so fast and now they were on their own in the world, and Símon was sure they'd been fed to the rottweiler who lived in an apartment on the ground floor. My uncle and father tried to calm us down, assure us that the pollitos were going to live long happy lives and be adopted by adult chickens that were lonely and wanted to be parents, but we were inconsolable. On top of it, our mothers were still giving each other the silent treatment. Mami was in one room saying, "I don't know why we bother coming here anymore," and Carmen was in another room muttering, "I don't know why she even bothers coming back."

Then the phone rang. It was one of the neighbors reporting some building gossip: Carla had been in a motorcycle accident. La pobre niña, the lady said, esta media muerta.

We went to see her at the hospital. Two days had passed and Carla was no longer half-dead but recovering, though her back was broken and she was wrapped in a long, thick plastic brace that made her look like a giant crustacean on the bed. Her arms were broken and her beautiful face was ripped open on one side, sliced by the concrete, though she said it was a milagro that that was all that had happened, since she hadn't been wearing a helmet, just that denim jacket her mother hated so much.

The novio was doing just fine. Somehow the guy made it out without a scratch and Carla's parents got to meet him in the hospital, and their first words to him were not hello but "She lost the baby." I know this much because all us kids were gathered around our parents' legs when they exchanged information.

Carla's mother, who was normally expressionless and always wore a tea suit, looked like she'd just been in an earthquake, and her father, a respected advertising man, looked like Carla was already gone. My father kept saying thank God she's all right, but her parents looked like they were ready to bury Carla and I didn't understand why.

When they let us in to see her, I held Carla's hand and told her she looked pretty, that the hospital light above the bed made her glow like an angel. Cris didn't come through the doorway and Símon was still traumatized from the missing pollitos and stayed on a plastic chair in the corridor with Sara looking over him, as usual. I told Carla I wished she were my sister. I always wanted a sister and all I got was lousy Cristían. Carla tried to laugh but her bones hurt, so she stopped. They hadn't yet told Carla she wouldn't walk again or that she would probably never have children of her own. That day, despite the stillness of her shattered body, Carla looked vibrant, her eyes dancing because Andy had just called to say he was on his way over to see her.

We left a few days later. I promised Carla I would write her letters, tell her all about my life in elementary school, let her know as soon as I got a boyfriend, and she promised she'd invite me to her wedding, though the last time I saw her, when we went over to the hospital to say good-bye, Andy was sitting all alone in a chair at the end of the hallway with his face in his hands. He didn't move from there during the full hour that we were with Carla.

Mami and Carmen finally made up, asked each other's forgiveness, and spent the whole last night of our stay sitting on the floor of the living room, going through photo albums of their childhood. There were no whispers from the other side of the wall that last night. Papi was snoring and Mami crept in without disturbing him, slipped under the heavy blanket, and went to bed without a sound. I lay in the darkness, the song of Bogotá humming several stories below the window.

The next day at the airport, we said our good-byes. Emilio kept asking my father when we were coming back and Papi wouldn't give him a straight answer. I could tell that if it were up to Papi, the answer would be *never*. Mami was crying. Hugging her sister as if it were the last time. Cris and I huddled with our cousins, said "See you later" because we already knew they were coming to stay with us in New Jersey that summer.

Emilio took me by the hand and walked me a bit away from our family crowd for some private words. "This is your country," he told me. "For better or worse you carry its salt in your blood."

I told Mami what my uncle said as the plane lifted off and we watched the city shrink into the Andes. She looked tired, her face resting on her palm, her lips pale because she'd forgotten to put on lipstick that morning. She shook her head, said Emilio always went overboard trying to be poetic and I should only listen to half of what he says. She didn't lift her eyes from the window, even after the mountains melted under the thick clouds and the plane drifted into a sea of milky sky. And I felt foolish because, for a moment, I believed him.

ACKNOWLEDGMENTS

A lifetime of love and gratitude to my father, Richard Engel, the greatest artist I know, and my mother, Patricia García Engel, for her infinite faith. My profound thanks to my brother, Richard, Swati, Jocelyn and Farah, André Vippolis, Lucie and Bruno, Elicabeth and Louis, Nena, Hans, Constanza and Augustín, Norita, Katarina, Eleany Uribe, our departed Abuela Lucía and Abuelo Herbert, Walter, Alba, Herbie, Frank, my extended family across the United States and Colombia, Junot Díaz, Gabriele Corto Moltedo, Ronny Kobo, Ariana Zsuffa, Stella Ohana, Jackie Raqcer-Farji, John Lin, Lisa Coar, Alexandra and P. Scott Cunningham, Julia and James and Jude Lin, Pierre Duval, Sara Martinez-Diefenbach, Ana Maria Lozano, Szabi Dobos, Carlos Delatorre, Dana Leven, Uzodinma Iweala, Matías Ventoso, Michele

Esteves, Frijol Sanchez, Liz Curtis, Amanda Espy, Sandra Vega Louit, Alexandre João Dias, Chris Abani, Sharline Chiang, Lizz Huerta, Christine Lee Zilka, Xhenet Aliu, Jennine Capó Crucet, Bob Wister, Lynne Barrett, Les Standiford, Margaret Porter Troupe and Quincy Troupe, Maryse Condé, David Mura, Diem Jones, Voices of Our Nations Arts Foundation, Key West Literary Seminar, the Hedgebrook Foundation, Bread Loaf Writers' Conference, Florida International University, and the Florida Division of Cultural Affairs. I am deeply grateful for the dedication of my agent Ayesha Pande, the passion and vision of my editor Lauren Wein, and the support of Morgan Entrekin and the Grove/Atlantic team.

Thank you for believing.

Vida

Patricia Engel

ABOUT THIS GUIDE

We hope that these discussion questions will enhance
your reading group's exploration of Patricia Engel's
Vida. They are meant to stimulate discussion, offer new
viewpoints, and enrich your enjoyment of the book.

More reading group guides and additional information,
including summaries, author tours, and author sites
for other fine Grove Press titles, may be found on
our Web site, www.groveatlantic.com.

QUESTIONS FOR DISCUSSION

1. Sabina is the recurring character throughout *Vida*, even when the point of view of the narration changes; we see her at different ages, in different cities, with and without her family, in different relationships. What do we come to learn about Sabina throughout the book? What kind of a girl or a woman is she? What is her relationship with her parents like? With her brother? With her Colombian identity? How does Sabina see herself, and the various roles available to her, in relation to the women in her own family? Consider her mother, her aunt Paloma, and other members of her extended family in the United States and in Colombia.

2. What do you make of the author's epigraph: "In each life, particularly at its dawn, there exists an instant which determines everything." Do you agree with this statement? Was there an instant in Sabina's life that determined everything?

3. At the end of "Lucho," Sabina realizes her true feelings for Lucho only after he dies: "I didn't even know I loved Lucho till that second. But I did . . . He came looking for me when I was invisible" (p. 22). How did Lucho

"come looking" for Sabina? How was she invisible? Many characters in this book die. What do you think the author is saying about life considering the various ways her characters experience death?

4. In "Refuge," Sabina mentions a coworker, Wanda: "Wanda likes me because we have the same last name though we are no relation—she's Puerto Rican and I'm Colombian stock—and she says us Latinos have to stick together though she doesn't speak Spanish" (p. 32). Ethnic identity is complicated; how does Wanda define ethnic identity? How does Sabina? Does Sabina agree that she and Wanda should "stick together"?

5. On page 35, a character says, "The guy is dead. And death is a huge aphrodisiac." Why could death be an aphrodisiac? Are there other examples in the book of love as a result of a certain kind of fantasy?

6. In "Refuge," Sabina's boyfriend Nico gets into a fight. "'The punches I took for you,' Nico would say, like it was a debt to be paid" (p. 39). Where else in this book are women considered to "owe" a debt to men?

7. In "Refuge," newspapers are hidden from children so that they won't see the disturbing images of 9/11. In "Lucho," Sabina's mother hid newspapers with information about the uncle on trial. What do you think of this separation of family/domestic life and the "news" of the world? Is it important or damaging?

8. Also in "Refuge," Sabina says, "It will be months, and most of the wreckage will have already been cleared, before we admit it's not enough. It will be uneventful, the way most life-changing moments are" (pp.43–44). After the aftermath of 9/11, Sabina and her boyfriend decide to break up. Do you agree with Sabina's statement that most life-changing moments are not the biggest events, but smaller ones? Has your personal life ever been significantly altered by an event that occurred on the world stage?

9. In "Green," the narration shifts and the story is written in the second person, although it's clear that the story is still being told from Sabina's point of view. What do you make of this shift in narration? How does it change—if at all—how you read?

10. On page 53, the narrator says, "Your parents are immigrants who don't really understand the concept of depression." What do you think about this statement? Is depression a particularly "American" phenomenon?

11. "I gave you a little smile so you would feel absolved" (p. 106). Guilt and blame come up frequently in the book—between couples who may or may not be faithful; in the aftermath of accidents; in friendships. What do you think of Sabina's sense of accountability—is she too frequently feeling guilty? Not enough? What about the other characters and their sense of accountability?

12. "He was a boyfriend for the shadows" (p. 122). Sabina has many secret-boyfriends or almost-boyfriends. Why do you think this is? What is it about these sorts of relationships she finds appealing?

13. Sabina tends to surround herself with other young drifters who spend their time looking for love and then fleeing from it. Discuss some examples of this tension between being sought out, being found, and the urge for isolation, retreat, escape.

14. Many different languages appear in the book—Spanish, Ukrainian, Portuguese, Hungarian. Even the Spanish is

not always the same to each character: "She found my Spanish amusing. Said I talked like it was the seventies. That's the Spanish my parents left with" (p. 120). What do you think of this cacophony of languages and second languages and translations? Do you think they ultimately lead to misunderstandings or does there seem to be an essential understanding among the characters, despite language barriers?

15. In "Vida," Sabina learns that a friend of hers had been forced to work in a brothel. Her reaction to learning this information about her friend is complicated. At first she feels she must keep it secret, because she fears that if Vida's boyfriend found out the truth, he would leave her. Then she learns that Vida's boyfriend had actually worked at the brothel with her. Sabina seems uncertain what to do; she claims at first she had no impulse to get involved: "Nothing in me said I should help Vida. . . . I just wanted to drink her up like everyone else" (p. 135). It's a question of exploiting Vida's story; when we learn of gruesome events, is our interest driven by a desire to help or by mere curiosity? Later on, Sabina accuses Vida's boyfriend of not helping her enough: "Being a witness can make a person just as guilty" (p. 141). Who is Sabina really accusing here?

16. Vida says, "There is no love. Only people living life together. Tomorrow will be better" (p. 145). What do you think of Vida's outlook on life and love? Is it optimistic or pessimistic (Or realistic?). Does Sabina share this outlook?

17. *Vida* moves back and forth from New Jersey to Manhattan to Miami, and then, finally, to Colombia, in "Madre Patria." What is Sabina's connection to Colombia? How does it differ from that of her parents'?

Suggestions for further reading:

Drown by Junot Díaz; *Last Evenings on Earth* by Roberto Bolaño; *War by Candlelight* by Daniel Alarcón; *How the Soldier Repairs the Gramophone* by Saša Stanišić; *The Question of Bruno* by Aleksandar Hemon; *Esther Stories* by Peter Orner; *The House on Mango Street* by Sandra Cisneros; *Book of Clouds* by Chloe Aridjis; *War Dances* by Sherman Alexie; *Miles from Nowhere* by Nami Mun; *Sightseeing* by Rattawut Lapcharoensap; *The Boat* by Nam Le; *Paraiso Travel* by Jorge Franco